ROOM AT HERON'S INN

Ginger Chambers

CHIVERS

British Library Cataloguing in Publication Data available

This Large Print edition published by AudioGO Ltd, Bath, 2012.
Published by arrangement with Harlequin Enterprises II B.V./S. à r.l.

U.K. Hardcover   ISBN   97814713 1078 2
U.K. Softcover   ISBN   97814713 1079 9

Copyright © 2011 Ginger Chambers
Originally published as *Till September*,
copyright © 1994 by Ginger Chambers

Printed and bound in Great Britain by
MPG Books Group Limited

ROOM AT HERON'S INN

Dear Reader,

Home, family, community and love. These are the values we cherish most in our lives — the ideals that ground us, comfort us, move us. They certainly provide the perfect inspiration around which to build a romance collection that will touch the heart.

And so we are thrilled to have the opportunity to introduce you to the Harlequin Heartwarming collection. Each of these special stories is a wholesome, heartfelt romance imbued with the traditional values so important to you. They are books you can share proudly with friends and family. And the authors featured in this collection are some of the most talented storytellers writing today, including favorites such as Brenda Novak, Janice Kay Johnson, Jillian Hart and Patricia Davids. We've selected these stories especially for you based on their overriding qualities of emotion and tenderness, and they center around your favorite themes — children, weddings, second chances, the reunion of families, the quest to find a true home and, of course, sweet romance.

So curl up in your favorite chair, relax and

prepare for a heartwarming reading experience!

Sincerely,
The Editors

CHAPTER ONE

The video image of a young girl, wrapped in a blanket and shivering, flickered upon the silent computer monitor. Her dark hair was soaked — long tendrils trailing across her face and shoulders and hanging down her back. Her equally dark eyes, prominent in her face, were wide with shock. A woman hovered next to her, her fingers wrapped around the child's thin arm as both watched the flurry of activity that was taking place a short distance away.

The footage then focused on the source of the activity, the camera's jerky movements and poor focus the sign of an unprofessional hand. Blobs evolved into members of a rescue team. Their bodies taut, their expressions intent, the group of men and women tried desperately to revive a man lying on the sand. When it became apparent that life could not be forced back into the flaccid form, all but one person gave up and turned away. The one person continued to try . . . until he, too, was forced to admit defeat.

The camera edged closer, the lens peering over the shoulder of the determined rescuer. The shot provided an excellent view of the victim. Even in repose his middle-aged body looked lean and athletic, his rugged features vital. A white long-sleeved shirt was plastered wetly to his skin, revealing the undershirt beneath. Gray pants clung to his legs; a dark sock covered one foot. A tiny gold medal, dangling from a chain on his neck, was partially lost in his thick, silver blond hair.

The image jiggled and swerved, as if the camera had been pushed away by an angry hand. An expanse of overcast sky, the same shade of gray as the Pacific, fought with shadows before the picture settled back onto the woman and the girl. In a close-up, the woman was shown biting her lip, while the girl, seemingly unable to take in what had happened, continued to stare straight ahead.

Abruptly the picture changed, gaining color and professionalism. The shot was of a large family huddled on and around a wide couch in a nicely appointed living room. The group ranged in age from toddler to early twenties. One child, a boy of about eight, started to sob as he reached for his oldest brother, the only adult on camera.

As always, the piteous sound tore into Robin's heart, and she groped for the mouse to cut off the boy's sobs. But a simple click couldn't stop the sound in her head. The echo went on and on. . . .

Robin covered her ears in a vain attempt to muffle the noise, just as she tried to erase the picture emblazoned on her brain — the sight of the man lying motionless on the sand. The man whose strong arms had once encircled her, dragging her to safety. She remembered the warm, reassuring look in his pale blue eyes as he said, "You're fine. Relax. I've got you now. I won't let anything bad happen to you."

His last words. Said with a smile.

She began to rock back and forth. She could almost feel his strength again as he fought against the pounding waves, carrying her with him, preventing her slight body from crashing against the vicious rocks by offering himself instead.

Time stopped as he battled the elements. The water was so cold Robin could barely feel her hands and feet, could barely move her legs. But she gamely tried to help. She tried, because he had lent her some of his courage.

The undercurrents worked against them, dragging them farther from shore, teasing them by letting them get close again. She remembered slipping below the surface, and then, them both going under. She remembered bursting into the air and being tumbled onto the rocks. She remembered feeling panic when his arms no longer held her. She remembered seeing him struggle toward her . . . then another huge wave hit.

After that she didn't remember much. She didn't remember the people who had found them or the rescue team that rushed to the scene. Her only memory of that time came from this film. She was like a person standing outside herself, viewing what had happened as if she were a third party, uninvolved.

She drew a trembling breath and clicked the play icon again. The child's sobs resumed, but this time Robin didn't flinch.

A reporter pushed a microphone into the eldest son's face. "You all must be very proud of your father," she said with forced good cheer, a style so evident among even some of today's reporters. Sixteen years hadn't changed much. "He's a hero to people all over the country."

The son, who looked a younger version of the man Robin remembered so clearly, tightened his lips as he glanced sharply at someone off camera. "We are," he agreed.

"I understand the governor is planning to call . . . to offer his condolences."

"We hadn't heard."

"Yes! I'm surprised he hasn't contacted you yet. Our sources at the Capitol tell us the call could come at any moment." She aimed the mike at another of the children, a girl of about ten. "What do you think, Allison?"

"Her name is Barbara," the oldest brother rasped, leaning forward. "And I'd really appreciate ending this right —"

The reporter stood up, cutting him off. "Yes," she said, smoothing over the difficulty by pretending to talk to the anchorman at the distant television station. "Yes, we'll be standing by, Frank. When the governor calls, we'll be sure to listen in. This is Jade Patrick for Channel 8 News, from the home of Martin Marshall, a true hero of our time. A man, who only this morning, sacrificed himself in order to save the life of a young stranger, and in the process left his own six children orphaned. Back to you, Frank."

The camera panned from the reporter to the faces of the children. Most of them looked stunned, as if they, too, were having a hard time grasping the significance of what had occurred.

There had been no other interviews. The oldest brother must have followed through with his determination to end any further intrusions into the family's grief. If there had been other interviews, Robin would have had them. Her father had searched high and low for everything concerning her rescue. Years ago he'd converted all the old snippets of film onto one CD.

Robin played the rest of the files. She saw vignettes from the man's well-attended funeral, from the ceremony a week later in which the governor declared that day Martin Marshall Day, from the ceremonial presentation in the White House Rose Garden when the president awarded the man a posthumous medal for heroism and presented it to his children. She watched as the story was revisited years later when a child lost his life along the same stretch of rugged coastline after a rogue wave washed ashore to pluck him from the beach, just as one had done with her. That child hadn't had a guardian angel watching over him. A guardian angel named Martin Marshall.

Silence reclaimed the apartment when the last clip ended. Robin sat motionless. At times it seemed as if it all had happened to someone else. She wasn't the bedraggled twelve-year-old girl on the beach, shaken and afraid, shocked by what had occurred, watching as her rescuer's life seeped into the sand. She was someone else: the person who had "gone on with her life," as the psychologist her mother had insisted upon sending her to had encouraged her to do. Who had gone back to school, laughed and played with her friends. Who had graduated from high school and attended college for a year before deciding that she wasn't cut out for academia and enrolled instead in a culinary institute. San Francisco, Paris, New York . . . she'd studied with some of the best chefs in the world.

But all the time this film was witness to the fact that she wasn't fully what she pretended. Particularly the section shot by an amateur who'd just happened to be on the beach that day. She played it often. Too often, her mother criticized. She didn't think it healthy for her only child to dwell upon the past.

While growing up, Robin had run the clips in secret when her parents were away from the house. After her father's death, as her mother prepared for a move back to her childhood home in Vancouver, Robin had promised faithfully to destroy all the files.

She'd even taken the CD outside, dropped it in a container and lit a match. But she couldn't bring herself to follow through. She retrieved the CD and hid it, as if it were a guilty secret to be reclaimed whenever she felt the urge.

She clicked on the first file and played it again, this time concentrating on the faces of the children. She knew their features as well her as own. Press clippings had told her their names: Allison, Barbara, Samantha . . . Eric, Benjamin, David. She'd never met them. Neither her parents nor the psychologist thought it a good idea. And later, she'd hesitated to make contact herself. What could she say? *Hello, I'm the person your father lost his life to save . . . and I'm sorry.* She doubted that would go over very well.

She moved to the window that overlooked San Francisco Bay. On a clear day, the fabled city shone like a jewel on the jut of land across the water. Today the view from her apartment, nestled high in the Berkeley hills, was obscured by fog. Great gray fingers had crept inside the Golden Gate and covered the area like a blanket.

She knew she shouldn't feel guilty. The wave that had tried to wash her out to sea was a freak of nature. It was known to happen where she'd been playing, but with such rarity that she couldn't be blamed. She had been walking along the beach, innocently searching for sand dollars, when . . .

She spun away from the window, from her memories both real and on film. A decision needed to be made. A decision she had been putting off.

She crossed the room to the black lacquered credenza, decorated with a delicate, hand-painted Chinese design on its doors, and reached inside for a folded section of newspaper. She took it with her to the couch.

"Wanted," the ad read. "Cook for summer, good pay, room and board, experience required," and it listed the name of an inn and a phone number.

Robin reached for the telephone. Seconds later a resonant male voice answered her summons. "Heron's Inn."

Her first instinct was to hang up. What was she doing? Was she crazy?

The masculine voice repeated its greeting, this time with a shade of irritation.

Hang up? Hang in? Robin drew a ragged breath. "Uh — yes," she murmured. "I'm, uh, calling about the ad you have in —"

She wasn't allowed to finish. "I have some time available tomorrow afternoon," he interrupted. "Can you be here?"

Light perspiration covered Robin's body. She felt both chilled and overheated.

"Well? Can you?" the man repeated.

Things were moving too fast! But what had she expected? She had made the first move. "Uh, yes — yes. What time?"

"Four o'clock?"

"That sounds good to me."

"All right. Four it is. Don't be late."

A click sounded in her ear. He had disconnected.

Slowly, Robin let the phone slide back into place. Well, she'd done it. There'd be no more waffling. Had she wanted to hear that the position was filled? She didn't know.

She looked at the glass-domed clock on the mantelpiece. Four o'clock tomorrow afternoon, he'd said.

She couldn't sit still. She walked jerkily back to the credenza and returned the newspaper to its hiding place, as if out of sight it would be out of mind.

She checked the clock again. She had told Marla she'd be in to work early that day. A new vendor was coming to show them his special cucumbers in hopes that they would meet the restaurant's exacting standards. Le Jardin enjoyed a national reputation for its unique and creative uses of a wide array of fresh vegetables. Marla Simpson was the owner of the restaurant and responsible for creating the menu in consultation with Robin and Jean-Pierre, the executive chef.

Robin had been with the restaurant for three years. As sous chef, it was her job to facilitate food preparation, to make sure that the kitchen was running smoothly and that all dishes met with Jean-Pierre's approval. She would hate to leave. But she couldn't expect Marla to hold her job open or for Jean-Pierre to shoulder the extra responsibility for any length of time.

Her friends would urge her not to do this. She had a great position, working at a place she loved with people she enjoyed. Her days were challenging, uplifting. And she was preparing to throw it all away because of something that haunted her from the past. The past was the past, they would say. Let it rest.

Undoubtedly wise counsel. But just as she couldn't make herself drop the match to destroy the CD, she couldn't ignore the ad that had been placed in the small north coast newspaper that she'd picked up on a whim while out driving two weeks before.

Martin Marshall's family needed someone to help prepare meals at their inn on Dunnigan Bay. She was qualified — overqualified. Dunnigan Bay wasn't exactly at the top of the list of tourist destinations. The area was too isolated for any but the most determined vacationer. When the family had settled there shortly before her departure to Europe, she'd wondered why they had chosen such a place. She had yet to find an answer to that question.

Heron's Inn. She liked the name, and wondered if the inn was profitable. Her head lifted with a jerk. How much time had she wasted? Her mind was in just as much of a fog as the Bay outside. She had to hurry!

As she changed from casual clothes into more suitable working attire, she thought about the person who'd answered her call. Was he one of the Marshalls? And if so, which one? Eric was the oldest, the one who had looked so tightly coiled on film. Was it Eric she would be meeting tomorrow? His direct manner on the phone suggested that possibility. She must remember, though, that all of the younger children had grown to adulthood in the intervening years, just as she had done.

She fastened a belt around her narrow waist, added a pair of onyx earrings, located her purse and hurried out to her car. The engine sprang instantly to life.

On the road, her mind again wandered. Why was she doing this? What did she expect to accomplish? Would she dare tell them who she was? The whole idea was bizarre. Did she think that by meeting them she could effect some kind of change? Their father had *died* because of her. She couldn't bring him back, no matter how badly she might want to. Or rather, was this some sort of self-imposed penance? Regardless of what her parents or her psychologist had told her, she knew instinctively that in order to go on, she had to go back. Like it or not, they shared a common link. And because of that link, the Marshalls were as much a part of her life as she was of theirs.

CHAPTER TWO

Heron's Inn nested comfortably among two short rows of clapboard Victorian houses that would have been right at home in a nineteenth-century New England fishing village. The main street — the tiny hamlet's only paved road — ended abruptly in the blue waters of the Pacific, with only the remnants of what once must have been a highly used docking area to give warning.

Dunnigan Bay itself was breathtaking in its quiet beauty. Tucked in a natural cove carved from the bordering cliffs and rugged hills, the bay seemed to have been crafted by a master's hand, a place of respite along the craggy coast. Clusters of windswept cypress trees were arranged in perfect balance, while twin pillars of weathered rock stood offshore in resolute defense of the bay's narrow entrance. A short beach glistened in the sunlight.

Robin waited nervously in her car, the

peacefulness of the beauty around her unable to penetrate the tension that had been mounting over the past twenty-eight hours.

This was not her first occasion to see Heron's Inn. She'd driven by it several times since her return to California, but she'd never stopped. Now she was about to go inside.

Her gaze darted to her wristwatch. It was time.

She stepped out of the car and straightened her skirt. The decision of what to wear had given her fits. She couldn't look either too successful or too desperate. She'd settled on a neat black skirt, a charcoal-and-white pin-striped blouse, black tights and a red pullover sweater to guard against the coastal chill. With her dark brown hair stylishly brightened with golden highlights and cut to skim the top of her shoulders, she might well have been the college student she'd decided to pretend to be.

The door on the landing opened and a couple stepped outside. Arms entwined around each other's waists, they spared little attention for anyone or anything outside of themselves. As if walking on a carpet of delicately scented rose petals, they drifted down the steps, along the pathway, past the gate in the low white picket fence and out to the street. Robin doubted if they even knew she was there. She watched as they turned toward the beach.

"Love's Splendid Young Dream," a male voice commented sarcastically from behind her.

Robin spun around to face the man who had come to stand in the doorway. Tall, leanly muscled, in his late thirties, with thick blond hair and rugged features — Robin recognized him instantly as Eric Marshall.

"Are you the cook?" he demanded without ceremony.

"Um . . . yes."

A half-smile lightened his expression. "Then come on. Let's get started."

Robin had a hard time making herself move. It was one thing to form a plan of action and another thing entirely to begin it.

He waited, holding the door open. Robin started forward. The closer she got, the more she wanted to turn and run. What did she think she was going to accomplish here?

"This way," he said after she crossed the threshold.

Robin gained a quick impression of nicely furnished rooms on either side of the wide entryway. A polished hardwood floor continued down the long narrow passage to the rear of the house. At its end, the high-ceilinged kitchen retained the flavor of a bygone era. Nicely preserved, it included a great old cooking range, wide marble countertops and an antique oak buffet that took up a large portion of one wall. Modern amenities had not been rejected, though. Another glance revealed a late-model mixer, a microwave oven and a dishwasher. The walls and cabinets had been freshly painted, while a set of French doors opened onto a small backyard garden.

"What's your name?" he asked, leaning back against the nearest section of counter.

"Robin," she said. "Robin McGrath." That wasn't completely the truth. Robin was a nickname she'd gone by all her life, and McGrath was her mother's maiden name. If she used her real name, he would know immediately who she was.

"Well, Robin, I'm Eric Marshall — part owner of this establishment, along with being the manager. Now, what I'd like is for you to show me what you can do."

"Do?" she repeated.

"Eight hungry people are going to show up in exactly one hour, all wanting their dinner. I promised them a good meal." His eyes, the same pale blue color as his father's, moved over her as if in assessment of her ability. "You haven't come under false pretenses, have you? You really can cook?"

"Of course! But I thought — don't you want to see my references? Or to hear anything about my training?" Not that she was going to tell him the truth along those lines, either. She'd spent most of last night coming up with what she thought was a good cover story. She'd even persuaded one of her friends who owned a trendy café in San Francisco's Marina District to back up her claim of having worked part-time for him.

"I believe in letting a person's work speak for itself. You'll find everything you need in the pantry and the refrigerator, and the freezer's through there in the utility room." He motioned toward a door across the room. "All we want is good, plain food served family style. Nothing fancy. Meat, potatoes, a vegetable. Maybe a pie or cake."

"An hour isn't very long," she cautioned him.

"If you can't do it, say so now."

"I can do it," she said, her chin lifting.

A wicked light began a dance in his eyes. "Let's hope so," he said before pushing away from the counter and leaving the room.

Robin released a long breath. This wasn't exactly the way she'd expected the interview to unfold. But his method wasn't all that unusual. She knew of a chef outside Paris whose test for a person wanting to learn from him was that person's ability to make a basic béchamel sauce. If the applicant could do it to his exacting standards, he or she was accepted as the great master's student.

Plain food, he'd said. Meat, potatoes, a vegetable. If that was what he wanted, that was exactly what she would give him. It would be good, and it would be on time.

She checked her watch and set about looking for ingredients.

No one disturbed her during the hour. She heard people moving about inside the inn, going up and down the stairs, opening and closing doors, raising their voices in greeting and in good-natured disagreement. Several times someone laughed. But no one came into the room, not even to check if she was still there.

Finally, as she adjusted the delicate seasoning of a dill cheese sauce, a young woman appeared as if from nowhere. It was easy to see that she was another Marshall. She shared the same long athletic body type, the same pale blue eyes, the same proud straight nose, well-defined cheekbones and square jaw. On her, though, the look was softer. Thick blond hair fell halfway to her waist, bouncing in a riot of soft unruly curls. A handful of hair had been swept away from her face and caught in a clip at the back of her head.

She grinned when she saw Robin's startled look. "Oops! I forgot. You don't know about the kitchen's back stairs. They're servant stairs, actually, from when this house was a private residence. It usually scares people to death the first time it happens. They think you're a ghost or something!"

"Well, it was a bit of a surprise," Robin admitted, turning back to her sauce. She felt, rather than saw, the young woman come across the room.

"I'm supposed to see if the meal is ready," she explained. "Eric is busy. He's on the phone." She lifted the lid on steaming broccoli and peeked into the oven at the browning roast. "Mmm," she approved. "It certainly smells good. Would you like me to set the table?"

"Would that interfere with the test?"

"Not at all," she said. "I almost always set the table." She started to pull dishes from the huge old buffet. "My name is Samantha, by the way. I'm Eric's sister. He tried to convince me to be the cook for the sum-

26

mer, but I wouldn't do it. I can turn out a fairly good meal when pressed, and people seem to like it. No one dies or anything. But to do it every day? No, thank you! I'd rather scrub floors."

Robin conjured a mental picture of the young Samantha. The girl had been five at the time of the accident, which meant she was now twenty-one.

"Cooking every day isn't that bad," Robin murmured. "I look upon it as a challenge."

Samantha pulled a face. "Like other people get off on working in an office from nine to five. No thanks. That's not for me, either!"

The girl carried the stack of dishes through a swing door into the adjoining room, leaving Robin to dish up the food.

"It's time to serve the meal, isn't it?" Robin asked when the girl returned for silverware.

Samantha nodded. "Everyone's in there except Eric and David." Her expression dimmed suddenly but quickly cleared again. "I'll remind Eric to hurry."

Robin used the next few minutes to lightly dress the meal. She arranged the sprigs of fresh basil she'd found growing in the garden around the roast, placed a square of butter in the center vortexes she'd drawn in twin bowls of mashed potatoes, and ladled a little of the cheese sauce over the two carefully arranged plates of broccoli. Not up to Le Jardin standards but definitely in keeping with her "just plain food" directive.

Samantha burst back into the kitchen, again by way of the rear stairs. "Eric's on his way. Here, let me help." Her eyes widened as she took in the dinner display, but she said nothing.

The dining room was filled by a long trestle table set in the center of the room and a half-dozen small tables lining the walls. Pristine white curtains, caught at half length, showcased a row of windows that overlooked the front and side yards. Place settings were laid only at the large table. Near the table's head, another young woman, again unmistakably a Marshall, gazed at Robin with undisguised curiosity.

Robin offered a quick smile and hurried back to the kitchen, murmurs of approval from those present already starting to sing in her ears. At the door, she almost collided with her prospective employer.

"Excuse me," he murmured, his hand shooting out to steady her.

"And me," Robin returned. She drew away unsettled, but didn't have time to question her reaction. She had rolls in the oven. If she didn't hurry they would scorch.

Her fingertips had been desensitized to heat long ago, and she didn't bother to search for a pair of tongs, not knowing if there even were any. She arranged the rolls on a platter and brought them into the dining room.

She was about to offer them to the diners when the front door closed with a loud bang. The Marshalls at the table stiffened, Eric most noticeably.

Heavy footsteps pounded across the entryway, then started up the stairs. Eric pushed back his chair and stepped into the hall.

"David," he said curtly. "You're late. Dinner is already on the table."

"I'm not hungry," a younger male voice growled in return.

"You need to eat."

"I said I don't *want* anything!"

"And *I* say . . . come to the table!" Cold anger lent Eric's softly spoken words a sharp edge.

Robin glanced at the two sisters. Their faces reflected their discomfort. The guests, however, were less concerned. The honeymoon pair continued to be aware only of each other, their bodies pressed together from shoulders to hips, as if resentful of the time and attention eating took away from each other. A retirement-aged couple seemed accustomed to what was happening and not unduly bothered by it, and the remaining elderly gentleman appeared more interested in his meal than anything else. Standing beside the elderly man, Robin offered him first choice of rolls.

Just then a teenage boy stomped into the room. His blond hair reached past his shoulders in a tumbled mass of defiance, and his Marshall features were set in anger. He wore torn black jeans, a faded black T-shirt on which a heavy metal rock band's emblem was barely visible and scruffy black motorcycle boots.

"Sit down and eat," Eric Marshall ordered gruffly as he accompanied the new arrival into the room.

Aggressive blue eyes flashed resentment, but the young man did as he was told, slumping noisily into the empty chair. He then tossed his head with enough vigor to jingle his single earring, and dug his tightly curled fists into his pockets.

Eric returned to his seat at the head of the table and replaced his napkin. His features were frozen. The sisters looked from him to their youngest brother, silently urging the latter to cooperate.

Robin made her way around the table with

the rolls, then slid the still half-filled plate into a vacant space.

"If this tastes as good as it looks . . ." Eric murmured as she passed beside him on her way back to the kitchen.

"It does!" Samantha cheered, seemingly grateful for anything that might defuse the tension. "The roast melts in your mouth, and this cheese sauce is to die for!"

"It's delicious," her sister agreed, and was seconded by the elderly gentleman.

"Are these rolls homemade?" the retirement-aged woman asked.

"Yes, they are," Robin confirmed.

"I thought so. If this is your new cook, Mr. Marshall, I congratulate you."

David squirmed in his chair, withdrawing his hands from his pockets only to fold his arms tightly across his chest. He must be close to his eighteenth birthday, Robin realized, but he was acting like a spoiled child.

Eric's lips tightened, though he gave no other indication that he had noticed David's failure to start serving himself. His eyes lifted to Robin's, and for a second she thought she saw a flash of pain.

Safely back in the kitchen, Robin leaned against the counter and closed her eyes. This was harder than she had thought it would be. Meeting them, talking with them . . .

31

Maybe she should back away. If he offered her the job, she could tell him that she wanted to think about it. Then, at a distance, she could refuse.

The timer rang, a reminder that she needed to start dessert. Normally, she liked to use fresh Bing cherries with this quick little bread pudding, but they seemed to have an over-abundance of apples, so that must mean apples were a favorite in this household. She made toast, which she then broke apart and soaked in a mixture of milk and apple jelly. Then she thinly sliced a half-dozen apples and ground up some almonds. Next, in individual custard cups, she layered the milk-and-jelly-soaked toast, the sliced apples, the almonds, then sprinkled sugar, cinnamon and a scant touch of nutmeg on top. She popped the cups into the oven for long enough to heat the puddings through, and seconds after removal served them to the waiting diners.

"Be careful," she murmured to each person in turn. "The cup is hot."

David's plate remained pristine, his arms still crossed in defiance. But as he watched Robin slide the apple dessert into place in front of the others, he sat up a little straighter. Robin winked at him as she served his cup. She received a startled blink in return.

Hiding a smile, she returned to the kitchen to wait. She busied herself by making more coffee and tea, in case the carafes she'd placed in the dining room became empty.

A short time later Eric joined her. "That," he said, "was superb. I honestly don't know how you did it in an hour."

"It's a little secret called a microwave oven. I partially cooked the roast before I switched it to the conventional oven. I'm not particularly fond of microwaves, but they do come in handy sometimes."

"If you still want the job," he said quietly, "it's yours."

She hesitated, remembering what she'd planned to do.

"It's just until the first of September," he continued. "Our regular cook is due back then." He paused. "If it's the money, I could up it a little."

"No, no, it's not that," she denied quickly, causing him to raise a whimsical eyebrow. "Well," she amended, "not *exactly* that."

"What is it, then?" he demanded.

"I thought . . . I mean to say . . . There's a class at the university that I found out about only this morning —"

A tap sounded on the swing door behind Eric. The sister who had yet to be intro-

33

duced to Robin peeked into the room. "I thought I heard voices," she explained as her brother moved out of the way. Her face had a maturity that Samantha's had yet to acquire. But she was not the thirty-two Robin knew the oldest sister, Allison, to be. So she must be Barbara, the one closest in age to herself. At the time of the accident, she'd been ten to Robin's twelve.

"I've offered her the job," Eric said, "but she seems to be having second thoughts."

Barbara looked concerned. "Oh, but — What have you been saying to her?" she demanded of her brother, then turned to confide to Robin. "Believe me, Eric's bark is much worse than his bite. We practically had to force Bridget to take the summer off. She's been planning this trip to Ireland for years, but she was afraid we wouldn't be able to cope without her. Especially Eric. She treats him like a favored son. 'I've saved a nice big piece of pie for you, Eric-my-boy. You're a fine, strapping lad. Go on, have a second helping!' " Barbara laughed. "It's a wonder you don't weigh a thousand pounds!"

Eric grinned at his sister's teasing. "You sound just like her."

"So," Barbara continued, smiling sweetly, "don't let Eric's rough exterior put you off.

If he growled at you, he didn't mean it. You'll absolutely love working here. The weather's wonderful, loads of peace and quiet, fabulous hiking trails. That's why people actually *pay* to stay here."

Robin felt herself caught up in Barbara's infectious goodwill. But before she could say anything, Eric murmured, "If it's David's behavior that upset you, I can't promise it will change. We have to be up-front about that. He's defiant and surly, just like any number of other kids his age, but generally he restricts his belligerence to me. I'm the only father figure he has."

Robin looked away. The reason Eric was the only father figure David had was because of her. If she had gone to the beach any other day . . . If she had noticed the huge wave's approach in time . . .

"He ate the dessert she made," Barbara put in.

"That's right," Eric agreed, "he did. Every bite."

Both of them waited. The ball was in Robin's court. Her gaze moved from one to the other, lingering longer on Eric. He returned her look levelly. Not only had the passage of years increased his resemblance to the man she remembered so well, but she sensed he possessed the same inner strength. He, too, would do whatever it took to deal with a situation. He had done it in the past and would do it again.

She started to speak but was forced to clear her throat. "All right," she agreed. "I'll do it." And she felt as if the weight of the world had suddenly descended upon her shoulders. Had she done the right thing? She wanted instantly to take the words back, but she couldn't.

"That's wonderful!" Barbara cried. She hugged Eric, then Robin, before running off to tell Samantha. The pair in the kitchen could hear her excited voice in the next room.

Robin moved uneasily, reaching out to switch off the coffeemaker. She felt Eric's eyes follow her.

"It really won't be so bad," he said. "We offer a continental breakfast, packed lunches if anyone requests them, then dinner. Your Mondays are free, and if anything else comes up, just tell us far enough in advance so we can make the proper arrangements. Bridget is due to return the end of August, and knowing her, she'll want to be back at the helm right away."

"That will be perfect for me, too. Are you sure you don't want my references? Most people —"

"I'm usually a fairly good judge of character. Between that and the meal you prepared, I don't have any questions left to ask."

Robin nodded. Because she was deceiving him, she had a hard time looking straight at him. "I'll clear the table," she said, and started toward the door.

He stopped her. "The girls will do that. Let me show you to your room instead."

As they walked to the front of the house, Eric told her a little of the small town's history. Shortly before the turn of the century, Dunnigan Bay had been a busy fishing village. Workers had come from the neighboring towns to man the boats that put out to sea. Then a scandal broke out, involving the owner of the fishing company. His devotion to profit eclipsed his concern for the well-being of his men. Several boats had been lost at sea due to poor maintenance and the pressure to stay out fishing, even in the face of intense storms. Numerous lives had been sacrificed. The remaining workers and the lost workers' families rightfully blamed Micha Talbot, the owner. They gathered outside his home, angrily swearing revenge. This home. The house that was now called Heron's Inn.

"What happened to him?" Robin asked.

"He slipped out a back window, made his way to the beach, stole a small boat and disappeared, never to be heard from again."

"How many fishermen died because of him?"

"Close to thirty."

"Does it bother you to live in a house with such an unsavory past?"

"All old houses have histories," he said. "About five families have lived here since Micha Talbot. All perfectly happy. No ghosts haunt it that I've ever seen."

Robin shivered lightly as she climbed the stairs in his wake. He glanced back at her and smiled. "You aren't superstitious, are you?"

"Not normally, no."

"Good. Bridget swears she's seen a shadow or two, but I think it's her Celtic imagination."

"Is this part of your being upfront with me?"

"Full disclosure," he teased. "No ghosts, just shadows."

"I'll remember that."

They reached the top of the flight of stairs only to start up another narrower and steeper set, which led to a third floor.

"The family lives up here," he said. "David, myself, Samantha and Barbara. That was Barbara you met last. She's scheduled to get married in about a month, so that will be one less mouth you'll have to feed. When he can, our brother Benjamin comes home for weekends. He's going to law school in San Francisco. Then there's Allison. She visits occasionally with her two children. That's no extra work for you, though. If the house is full, we all pitch in."

"You have a large family," she remarked, sensing that if she made no comment, the oversight would be noticed.

"Yes, I do," he agreed. "This way . . . to the end of the hall. When Allison and Benjamin aren't here, you'll have a bit of privacy. They have the closest bedrooms. When either of them are here, though . . ." He paused. "I hope you don't mind being thrown in with the family. Bridget has been with us for almost fourteen years and she feels at home. But if you object, we could —"

"No, this is fine. I don't mind," Robin interrupted. She'd wanted to get to know the family. What better way than this?

His expression relaxed. "Well," he said, opening the door, "here it is. The room's pretty much as Bridget left it. If you'd like to box up any of her things and put out your own, feel free."

The small room was filled with furniture — a double bed, two chests of drawers, a vanity table and chair, a wardrobe and a small writing desk.

"We don't run to closets in the place. It would cost a fortune to install them and Allison thought it added to the charm to have wardrobes. She held out for keeping everything as close to the original as we could have it, except for plumbing, of course. We do have a shower in the family area. Downstairs, we have only tubs. The guests seem to prefer that."

"Mmm," Robin murmured.

"So when can you start?" he asked.

"When do you need me?"

"Yesterday?" he joked.

"How about Monday? That's three days from now."

"You have Mondays off," he reminded her.

"I'll forfeit this first Monday. It will give me a chance to learn my way around."

"Deal," he said, and thrust out his hand.

Robin looked at it. It was long-fingered and capable, just as his father's had been. Even without the trigger of the video, she was propelled back into that terrible moment, when her rescuer had looked at her and told her that everything would be all

40

right. Well, it hadn't been all right. And she wasn't sure that it would ever truly be all right again.

CHAPTER THREE

"Do you think she'll be here soon?" Samantha asked as she carefully placed thick
turkey sandwiches into small plastic bags. "I
don't want to make dinner again this
evening. It's Barbara's turn, anyway, but she
and *Timothy* have something they have to
do. Honestly, I like the man, but if I hear
his name too many more times . . . And if I
hear too much more about the wedding . . .
I think they should have a little consideration and elope. That's what I'd do. Just up
and do it. No muss, no fuss. If it wasn't for
Eileen, that's what I think they'd do, too.
But she's so freaked. She needs to relax.
Not be so *intense* about everything. She
needs to be more like you." She directed a
quick look at Eric, who was packing the
sandwiches, fruit, chips and a thermos of
hot coffee into one of the medium-sized
wicker picnic baskets they kept for the use
of their guests.

Eric smiled. He enjoyed listening to Samantha's chatter. She could cover more subjects in one minute than most people could in ten. "She'll be here," he assured her.

His youngest sister sighed. "I miss Bridget. I didn't think I would so much, but I do. And not just because I miss her cooking. I miss her because . . . well . . . I'm glad she's having a good time, though. She wrote that Ireland was so green from the air. I hope she finds that cousin she's looking for. Are people really a cousin when they're so many times removed? A great-great-great-great-aunt's child? Will they look anything alike, do you think? Do we have anyone like that in our family? A rich cousin who's rumored to live in a castle?"

"If we do, I don't know them," Eric said.

"Maybe I should investigate our family history to see if *we* have any royal blood."

Eric laughed. "We're a family of brigands, most likely."

"Brigands!"

"We live on the seacoast and take people's money."

"They *give* us their money, willingly. And we give them a good time. Sometimes I wonder, though . . ." Her words drifted away.

43

"What do you wonder?" he prompted, still teasing, still enjoying her youthful exuberance.

"What our lives would have been like if Dad hadn't —"

Eric shut the wicker lid and fastened the clasp with a decided snap. "It doesn't do any good to wonder," he said brusquely. "Here. You'd better get this to the Petersons. After hiking to the Overlook, they might find they need a little more than love to get back on."

Samantha accepted the basket, but the wistful look didn't leave her eyes. "Don't you ever wonder, Eric?" she persisted.

"No," he answered firmly. "I'm too busy."

"What about love?" she asked. "Are you too busy for that, too? You always sound so . . . cynical, when you say the word."

Eric drew a deep breath. For sixteen years he'd done his best to be both mother and father to his siblings. He'd made mistakes, but he'd always tried. Patience was the virtue he'd had the hardest time learning. He took his sister by the shoulders, pointed her in the direction of the hall and gave her a little push. "I'll let you know when it's time to worry."

"But you'll be all alone soon," she protested, pausing at the door. "Barbara's get-

44

ting married, I'll probably be leaving in the next year, and David —" Nothing more needed to be said about David. David could easily disappear in a few weeks when he turned eighteen.

"Ah, blessed peace!" Eric exclaimed.

"I just want you to be happy," Samantha murmured.

Eric relented. He walked over to her and wrapped her in a big bear hug. "I know you do. That's what I want for you, too. For all of you."

Samantha managed to save the basket from being crushed. "Hey! Watch out!" she cried, giggling as she broke free.

Eric shook his head in amusement as he turned back into the kitchen, only to find that while Samantha had taken her leave, David had slunk into the room by way of the back stairs. The boy was dressed in his usual manner, the rips in his jeans a little more frayed than the day before. He acknowledged Eric's presence with a grunt.

"You're a little late getting started, aren't you?" Eric commented, his good humor suddenly evaporating. "Eleven o'clock isn't exactly the crack of dawn. Did Mrs. Wilson give you the morning off, or have you decided to play hooky?"

David threw him a hostile stare from

45

beneath a mass of tangled blond hair. There was every possibility that his hair *had* been combed . . . yesterday, the day before? He dug into the open plastic bread wrapper, withdrew a slice of bread and tore off a large chunk with his teeth — an action that he knew would send Eric around the bend.

Eric strove to maintain control. He understood exactly what his brother was doing. "I asked you a question," he said tightly.

"It's all a waste of time anyway," David groused. "I'm not about to go to college, so I don't see why I should have to spend time trying to —"

"You're in this situation now because you wasted so much time in school last semester. A little judicious studying then, and —"

"Yeah, yeah, yeah. So you've said before."

Eric's ire finally rose. "Whether you like it or not, David, you're going to make up that credit! And if Mandy Wilson is willing to work with you —"

"The woman's got something seriously wrong with her brain. She *thinks* in French, and she's not even French!"

"It's called knowing a language well."

"She expects *me* to think in French."

"Good!"

David's top lip curled, showing his disdain. "It'll never happen," he said softly, before tearing off another piece of bread.

Eric concentrated on clearing away the crumbs that had accumulated on the counter. "Another thing," he said after a moment had passed. "Our substitute cook is arriving today. I suppose you picked that up over the weekend?"

"Yeah, I heard," the boy said sourly.

"I don't want you to give her any trouble."

David laughed shortly and shook his head, as if completely incredulous that his brother could think such a thing.

"I mean what I'm saying, Davey," Eric warned.

"Don't call me that!"

"It's better than what I'd like to call you!"

David tossed what remained of his breakfast across the room, the crust of bread hitting the far wall before settling on the floor. Both brothers looked at it.

"Pick it up," Eric said quietly.

"You pick it up," David defied him.

Tension crackled tautly in the air between them when a hesitant tap sounded on the door frame at the hall. Reluctantly, Eric's gaze was drawn to the direction of the noise.

Robin McGrath stood just outside the kitchen, a look of uncertainty written on her face. Eric groaned. She'd had second thoughts before . . . what was she going to think now? She'd been the best by far of the three candidates he'd interviewed, and he couldn't afford to lose her.

"I knocked on the front door," she said, "but . . ."

She looked from one to the other. Any minute now and she would bolt. Eric forced himself into action. "It's perfectly all right," he said. "Come in. We were just —"

Eric stopped in midsentence as he saw his brother reach into the wrapper for another slice of bread, then start to saunter away from the disruption he'd caused. When he paused to smirk before he stepped into the hall, Eric's restraint snapped.

"Excuse me," he muttered, pushing past his newest employee to catch up with his recalcitrant brother.

The boy's walk was dripping with attitude. No doubt he thought he'd gotten away with something. To show him that he hadn't, Eric grabbed his arm and jerked him around.

"Look, you!" Eric said tightly, forcing the words through clenched teeth. "You go straight to Mrs. Wilson's house, apologize for being late and ask her if you can make up the lesson this afternoon. Then you get right back here and start pulling weeds out of the front flower beds. If you're not back in ten minutes, I'm going to come find you, wherever you are, and drag you back here. Understood? Life isn't a free ride, David. You don't have a ticket that entitles you to special treatment."

There was a time, years back, when David had looked upon him with love and respect. But even then there had been instances when the younger boy had turned in on himself and not let anyone close. Over the years those instances had intensified and lengthened, until they'd reached the point where David had come to hold him, Eric, responsible for everything that had gone wrong in his life. That was the message in his eyes now — aggrieved accusation.

Eric's jaw tightened at David's continued silence, but he didn't let go of his brother's arm. He couldn't. It was their only contact. "Did you hear what I said?" he demanded.

"Of course I did. I'm not deaf."

Eric wanted to shake him until his teeth rattled. He wanted to force some form of sense into him. *He wanted to build a bridge so that the two of them could talk again.* Instead, he let go of the boy's arm.

After brushing off his sleeve, David walked stiffly out of the house.

Mr. and Mrs. Brinkman appeared at the top of the second landing and started down the stairs. The retired couple were dressed for an afternoon of bird-watching. When they saw Eric, they smiled and greeted him warmly. Eric returned their greeting with automatic good cheer, then remembered the new cook and hurried back to the kitchen.

She hadn't wasted the time she'd spent waiting for him. The loaf of bread had been replaced in the bread box, the remaining crumbs on the counter had been removed, and the counter wiped clean. She also had washed the coffee beaker and the soiled flatware.

When she turned to look at him, Eric didn't know what to say. He hadn't expected such efficiency. Nor had he registered, until this moment, the full impact of her attractiveness. He had noticed that she was pretty, but not *that* pretty. Her eyes were the color of rich dark chocolate, at odds with the golden highlights in her hair. Her face was a perfect oval, her skin a creamy peach, her nose short and straight, her lips . . . She was wearing a simple cotton print dress and loose-fitting sweater that could easily have hidden her figure, yet somehow didn't.

Eric motioned to the counter. "You're off to a fast start."

"Yes." She seemed ill at ease, and who could blame her? The timing of her arrival had not been auspicious.

"David and I — we were just . . ."

She shrugged and looked away. "It's none of my business."

He released a short breath. She was right. He was searching for something else to say when Samantha burst into the room.

"Oh! Hello again!" the girl cried upon seeing Robin. "I didn't know you'd arrived! Eric was just asking when you'd get here." She winked at her brother, including him in her joke. "I told him not to worry, you'd be here soon, but I'm not sure he believed me."

Eric reproached his sister with a look. "That's not quite the truth," he defended himself. "I wasn't worried. I —"

Samantha laughed. "It doesn't matter now. She's here! Oh! I gave the lunch basket to the Petersons and made sure the Brinkmans had the proper directions to Russian Cove. I asked them if they wanted a lunch basket, too, but they said they planned to try out that little spot you told them about. The one that serves such great calamari and has all the bird paintings." She frowned. "I haven't seen Mr. Caldwell yet this morning. Have you?"

"He went off on his own about an hour ago," Eric answered.

"So we have the house to ourselves for a while. Wonderful! We can take Robin around

51

and show her the place without having to worry about anyone needing something. You don't mind if I call you Robin, do you? You can call me Sam, if you want. Eric doesn't like it when people shorten my name, but I don't mind."

A slightly bewildered smile flickered over Robin's lips. Eric knew that Samantha could be an overwhelming force, if a person wasn't prepared. "No," he put in, "*I'm* going to take Robin around and show her the place. *You* have something else to do, don't you?"

Samantha groaned. "But I hate to clean that mirror. Ever since Benjamin played that trick on me and —"

"It's either that or the bathrooms."

"I'll clean the mirror!"

"Good for you."

Eric took his new employee by the arm and gave a gentle tug. Her skin was warm, the flesh firm. She responded immediately to his prompting, which created a sensation deep inside him that he did his best to ignore as she preceded him out of the kitchen.

What a beginning, Robin thought as she walked stiffly down the hall. This wasn't going to work. She must have been mad to put herself in such a position. These people had lives they were happy in, or at least accustomed to. They had established a certain order, and her presence was potentially disruptive to that order. Maybe she should admit everything, turn to Eric Marshall right this minute and confess.

She turned around and he almost crashed into her.

"Be careful," he warned. "These halls can be dangerous. They're not quite as wide as in other houses."

She looked up into his laughing blue eyes and swallowed. "I need to tell you something," she confided solemnly.

His smile faded. "I was afraid you might."

Silence stretched. Words tumbled through her mind, but she couldn't say them. Instead she stammered, "I — my things. What do I do with my things?"

His relief was palpable, confirming how very badly the Marshalls were in need of help. She had sensed that same anxiety the last time she'd come here, but she had been so wrapped up in her own emotions that she'd barely remembered it, until now.

"Are your suitcases in your car?" Eric asked.

She nodded.

"Then how about if I go get them and

take you to your room. You can settle in, and I'll show you around the place later. There's plenty of time for that, really. Samantha gets overly excited about anything new. There's still a lot of kid in her."

He smiled again, and Robin was caught by his easy charm. It wasn't suave or practiced. It was just there, a part of him. She wondered if his father had had that same trait.

As she continued to look at him, a delicate tension began to build in the space between them, only to be broken when the front door opened a crack and David shouted inside, "I'm back! You don't have to come looking for me. Maybe we should invest in a time clock. But then slaves don't get paid for their labor, do they?" The door slammed shut on his last word.

"That boy is doing his best to scare you off, isn't he?" Eric murmured.

Again the tension began to grow, this time to be interrupted by Samantha. "Are you two still here?" she demanded as she erupted into the hall with a stepladder, glass cleaner and buffing cloth in hand.

"We're working on it," Eric countered. "Give us time." To Robin he said, "I'll get your things and be back in a minute. Is the car locked?"

54

"No," she said. He was gone before she could say anything else.

Samantha grinned. "Actually," she confided, "I told a fib earlier. I was the most impatient for you to get here. Not Eric. Not that he wasn't anxious, mind you. With the wedding coming up so soon, there's not a lot of extra hours in the day for any of us. Timothy's mother is doing most of the work, the planning and everything, but Eric has to go calm her down at least once every couple of days. She freaks about everything! I think she has a thing for Eric and creates these little panics just to get him to come see her. But he's determined to do his part. Big brother to the bride and all that."

Robin followed her into the formal living room, which, along with the dining room, comprised the two main rooms branching off the front entrance. The decor — overstuffed reading chairs and sofas, chests and tables, bookcases bulging with games, various types of reading matter, freshly cut flowers, and richly colored oriental rugs — was cheerfully inviting.

Samantha marched to an ornate mirror centered over the wide fireplace, positioned the stepladder securely in place, climbed confidently to the fourth rung, squirted the glass cleaner on the surface and started to rub. The ammonia made Robin's nose twitch.

The front door opened and Eric paused, holding her suitcases. The two leather cases had seen Robin through three years and two continents. At the moment they looked ready to burst, their sides bulging with all that she had brought. She was slightly embarrassed by their appearance.

"You remember the way, right?" he said, motioning her toward the staircase.

After retracing the path they had taken several days earlier, they walked to the rear of the third floor, where he shifted the suitcases to one side and ushered her through Bridget's door.

"We cleared some space for you, so you wouldn't have to do it yourself," he said. "A few drawers in the chest, some space in the wardrobe. But if you need more room . . ." He set the weighty cases down by the bed.

"I'm sure it will be fine," Robin said.

He lifted an eyebrow in doubtful amusement.

She walked to the window and looked outside. From this height she could see past the trees in the neighboring yard to a wide expanse of the Pacific Ocean. All her life she'd been drawn to the sea. It seemed to hold the key to the elements of her existence. Her past, her present . . . her future?

She let the curtain fall back into place and looked around to see that Eric Marshall had been steadily watching her. For a moment she'd forgotten that he was there. She smiled, hoping to cover her distracted state. It took a few seconds for him to return her smile.

"This is such a beautiful area," she murmured. "Do you have many visitors in the year?"

"Enough to keep the place functioning. A good many repeat customers."

"How many guests can you accommodate at one time?"

"We have seven rooms. Two king suites, two doubles and three with twin beds. The three twins have to share a bath down the hall. The most we support is fourteen people, give or take an extra person or two on occasion." She glanced wordlessly around the room.

"None of the rooms in the family quarters have private baths," he said, answering her curiosity. "When you're ready, I'll show you around. Take your time."

Robin wanted to claim that she was ready now. But a little time to herself would be nice, if only to draw a few unobserved breaths. "Would fifteen minutes be all right?" she asked.

"This is your free day, remember?"

"Fifteen minutes will be fine," she told him.

"I'll meet you in the family room."

"Where's that?" she asked, stopping him.

"Just turn right in the hall outside this door and keep going to the front of the house."

Once she was alone, Robin stood in the middle of the room, closed her eyes and waited for the seconds to tick slowly by.

Eric went downstairs to check on David. Miraculously, the boy was doing exactly as he'd been told: determinedly, if haphazardly, weeding the front flower bed. On his way back inside, Eric stopped by the living room, to find Samantha putting the finishing touches on the huge fireplace mirror. In Barbara's stead, he was supposed to clean and straighten the occupied rooms this morning, but full service would have to wait until he'd shown Robin McGrath around. As he'd said earlier, there was plenty of time to do everything. The two visiting couples would be away most of the day, as would Donal Caldwell. As usual, the elderly gentleman, who had been one of their first guests eight years before, had left the inn carrying his easel and paints. He would be away for the day.

Eric sprinted up the first set of stairs and into a suite and, with ease born of repeated practice, stripped the sheets from the over-size bed, replaced them with fresh ones, and shook the thick feather comforter back into place. After a quick repositioning of the pillows, he thought that he might have time to do the same thing to the next room down but he decided against it. He didn't want to make Robin wait.

She was already in the family room, looking at an old photograph of the six Marshall siblings. She'd been holding it with both hands, staring at it intently. When she became aware of his presence, she jumped and hastily replaced the framed photo on the table.

"Quite a crew, weren't we?" Eric mused with fond remembrance as he took time himself to examine the photo. He had a vivid memory of posing for this photograph. He remembered his father coaxing everyone from behind the camera . . . Allison at sixteen, attempting to hold the squirming two-year-old David . . . Benjamin at eight, teasing the five-year-old Samantha . . . Barbara at ten, melting into his best jacket, hiding her face in its sleeve. He'd been at college then, in his senior year. His father had taken any number of shots that morning, trying for a "keeper," as he called it. It was a difficult job to persuade such a disparate group to cooperate. Who would have thought that barely one month later . . . ?

Eric put the photo down and looked at his new employee. There was something strange about the way she returned his gaze, almost as if she knew what he was thinking. He frowned. Something certainly had gone off kilter for him this morning. He felt as if he'd been knocked out of position, and for some reason couldn't quite get back into step.

He gave himself a mental shake. Okay, so he was attracted to her. That didn't mean he had to concoct fanciful interpretations for her every act.

"Are you ready?" he asked, uncomfortably aware that an overcompensating briskness had stiffened his tone.

She seemed taken aback by his sudden change from newfound friend to detached employer, but she quickly took refuge in her own official status. "Of course," she said evenly setting her shoulders.

"I thought I'd start the tour by showing you some of the unoccupied guest rooms on the floor below. It's not necessary for your job, of course, but just in case you're curious . . ."

He paused at the door for her to precede him, and she spared him a cool glance as she went by.

CHAPTER FOUR

Robin sat on the end of the short pier, swinging her feet above the gently cresting waves. On occasion, a wave would build and tickle her bare toes before pushing on to shore. The water was cold, but refreshing in small doses.

At the base of the twin rock towers at the entrance to the bay, a sea lion barked to its companion, who glided sleekly through the water in search of food. Seabirds fought the chill breeze in the same pursuit.

A week had passed since her arrival. A week that had been both easy and difficult.

Robin leaned back, resting some of her weight on her outthrust arms, and lifted her face to the morning sun.

So far, the most trying aspect of her new job was to remember that in her present persona she wasn't an accomplished chef. She couldn't allow herself to perform any of the professional maneuvers that had become second nature. She had to proceed slowly and at times — at least, for her — awkwardly. She couldn't afford to show her true skills. She also had to keep the meals simple, ordinary. As time went by, possibly she could branch out a bit creatively, but that moment would have to be carefully tested.

Much more difficult to carry out were her personal dealings with the Marshalls. It wasn't easy to let herself be drawn into their lives, even though that was why she had come here.

Samantha had accepted her as readily as if she were a lost puppy the girl had found and given a good home. Her chatter was free, her heart open.

Barbara was more reticent, her personality quieter, although she had accepted Robin as a member of the household and had even proudly introduced her to Timothy.

While it was possible David had uttered a word to her this week, Robin couldn't recall what it was. He and Eric seemed to have regular altercations; each had an uncanny ability to get under the other's skin. So far, though, the boy had done nothing overt to strike out against her, and for that she was grateful.

Dr. Mays, the psychiatrist her mother had

taken her to as a child, would be appalled to learn what she had done. She had told Robin repeatedly that what had happened was not her fault. But how did a person escape such a feeling? You could run away, but the memory never truly disappeared.

Water splashed over her toes again, this time causing a chill. Robin pulled her feet back onto the pier, dried them and slipped on a pair of woolly socks and sneakers before rolling down her jeans.

She stood up, ready to start back to shore. But as she turned, she saw a familiar figure at the end of the pier. With his hands plunged deeply into his pockets, his long thin frame hunched, David seemed to be waiting for her. He glanced her way but looked quickly away again.

Robin hesitated, then closed the distance between them.

The boy was dressed in his usual faded black garb, his hair a mass of loose curls tangled by the breeze. Only now he had added a scuffed-up black leather jacket. His thin face had the stamp of a Marshall, though it was drawn with a less aggressive hand than his siblings' faces. There was a certain "unfinished" look about him that the next few years would probably resolve. He was young. Very young.

"I saw you sitting out there," he said after she had stopped a short distance from him. His tone was studiously casual.

"So you thought you'd come keep me company?"

His pale blue eyes were wary. "Not really," he said.

She grinned. "Too bad. I was hoping for someone to talk to."

David snorted. "Who wouldn't be bored in this place? There's nothing to do, nothing to see."

"It is quiet," she agreed.

He snorted again. "You don't know the half of it! Wait until you're here for a month or two. It'll drive you nuts, just like the rest of us."

"I didn't realize that all of you were —"

"Completely crazy. We live here, don't we? Other people come to visit, but we actually *live* here."

"And that's bad?"

"Awful!" he affirmed. "I liked San Francisco better. There was always something to do. My friends were there."

"You have friends here, don't you?"

He frowned fiercely. "Of course I do."

"Then —"

"It's not the same. Eric decided we'd move, so we moved. He didn't ask, he just told us." He paused. "I hate it here!"

"Have you told Eric how you feel?"

He wheeled around and started to walk away. She matched his pace. "He knows," he said sullenly.

They walked in silence along the steeply rising trail that led toward the Pacific.

"What made you come here?" he asked, once they had halted at the edge of the cliff. The wind, stronger now that they were away from the protected cove, buffeted their bodies and whipped their hair.

Robin thought the view reason enough. It was magnificent! Brilliant blue sky, equally brilliant blue ocean, crashing surf, the picturesque beauty of Dunnigan Bay, and farther beyond, the wild cragginess of the Pacific coastline. David, however, seemed blind to everything except his problems.

She shrugged and said lightly, "It seemed a good idea at the time."

"But it's a decision you regret. I don't blame you. Eric can be a real —" He swallowed the word he'd been about to use.

As the silence drew out again, Robin answered, "Actually, I don't mind working for him. He doesn't interfere. He lets me do my job."

"Maybe you haven't been here long enough. Just wait until you do something wrong, or what he *thinks* is wrong. Then you'll see."

"Barbara said Bridget gets along very well with him."

The boy made a quick dismissive motion. "Bridget thinks the sun shines out of his —" Again he censored what he was about to say, kicking some dirt with the toe of his motorcycle boot. "A lot of people do," he murmured instead. "Eric this, Eric that. Saint Eric!"

Robin turned to look at him. His young face was miserable. It reflected anger, resentment, deep unhappiness. Her heart twisted. That brother should harbor such animosity against brother . . . Would these feelings have occurred without the accident of their father's death forcing each into an artificial relationship? David had been two years old at the time. Some people didn't believe children that young could be affected by the happenings around them. By the looks of it, David had been, as well as by the difficult years that followed.

Robin searched for something to say. She wanted to help in whatever way she could. After all, it was because of her that — She forced her mind away from that line of thought. Assessing her own guilt was not the answer at this moment. She brushed strands of hair away from her face and changed the subject. If she was to be of any help to David, she had to gain his trust, and she didn't think the process could be hurried.

"I see you like Black Obsession." She indicated the faded emblem on the front of his T-shirt. "Are they your favorite band?"

David's face immediately brightened. "Yeah, they're great. Their last album was a killer! Especially 'Twin Delay.' I like the way Digby takes on the idiots who spend their lives thinking they can make a difference in the world, when everybody knows that they can't! They just keep running in their tiny little wheels like pet rats after some kind of imaginary —" He stopped abruptly, as if he'd suddenly realized he was providing too close a glimpse inside himself.

What Robin saw was a young man who was a much deeper thinker than he wanted other people to believe. Robin was familiar with the rock group he was talking about, and with that particular song, as well. Several of the line cooks at Le Jardin were fans of rock music and frequently received permission from Jean-Pierre to play the radio while they worked. That song did berate the do-gooders of the world, but the imagery David had used to describe this was his own. The boy had proved he was very articulate, particularly for someone who had had such a hard time in school — flunking subjects, spending inordinate amounts of time in detention and now in danger of not obtaining his diploma, if what she'd overheard was true.

"Yes," she said, "I like it, too. I'm not sure I completely agree with what Digby says, but I like the way he says it."

"You like it?" David echoed in surprise.

Robin smiled lightly. "I just said so, didn't I?"

The boy looked completely thunderstruck that someone quite a few years older than him had even heard of the band he loved so much, much less appreciated them. "But — but," he stammered, "Barbara and Allison, and even Sam, hate — and Benjamin, too. He —" He paused to regroup his thoughts. "They're a small band, not all that well-known. How do you know about them?"

"How did you learn about them?" she countered.

"On the radio."

"Can't I listen to the radio, too?"

"But to the kind of station that plays Digby . . ."

She turned away to move back down the trail. This time it was David who fell quickly into step beside her. "You're different," he said after several silent moments.

"Is that a compliment?" she asked.

He shrugged. "I suppose."

She glanced at him. His face had lost some of its defiant anger. She had broken through, if only temporarily.

"David!" a sharp, angry voice called.

David and Robin looked up to see Eric standing at the end of the trail. The boy tensed and the sullen look instantly returned to his face.

"David, what did I ask you to do earlier?" Eric demanded.

The boy said nothing.

Eric provided his own answer. "I asked you to pick up a package in Vista Point. Why haven't you done it?"

"I don't know," David grumbled.

"Well, I'd appreciate it if you could find the time to do it now, before you have to go over to Mrs. Wilson's for your lesson. Do you think you can do that? I mean, it wouldn't be too much of an imposition?"

The sarcasm wasn't lost on David. His lips narrowed and his fingers curled. But before he could form a hateful reply, Robin said, "David was showing me around. I'm sorry if I kept him from doing your errand. I didn't mean to get in the way."

Eric's pale blue eyes focused on her, and Robin could feel the tension mount within her, as well. During the past week, they had both scrupulously kept to their roles as employer and employee. There had been no private exchanges since her first day, no more odd little sparks of surprised awareness. Thinking back, Robin wasn't even sure that those sparks had occurred in the first place. But the mere possibility that they had made her uncomfortable in his presence. Her sensors automatically leapt to first-stage alert whenever she was near him, and there didn't seem to be anything she could do to shut them off.

"David should have told you he had a job to do." His gaze moved back to the boy.

"I didn't think you'd want me to be rude."

"Since when has that stopped you?" his brother snapped.

Robin hated to hear them argue. "Please," she broke in. "I didn't mean to cause trouble. I wish —"

David bulldozed over her last words. "There! Are you happy? You've made her feel bad." He shook his head in mock disgust. "Why don't you show a little consideration for other people, Eric? It's what you tell me all the time."

"Please . . ." Robin repeated.

She could see that David's hectoring was beginning to get under Eric's skin. Still, he managed to hold on.

"Maybe you'd better get going," he suggested tightly.

David had no trouble picking up on the warning yet he clung to an edge of cocky bravado. "Yes, all right," he agreed, "I will. But not because you tell me to. I'm going because I don't want to see Robin upset any more than she already is. She didn't ask for this. All she wanted was someone to talk to."

With that, he swaggered off down the street toward the inn. A few moments later, a late-model SUV backed out of the driveway and sped away, leaving behind a rooster tail of dust.

Robin moved to the edge of the pier and sat down again. Only this time she sat with her ankles crossed and her arms wrapped tightly around her drawn-up knees. She stared at the water and began a gentle rocking. Her emotions were a jumble. As an only child, she wasn't accustomed to arguments between siblings. This, however, went far beyond a simple argument.

She became aware that Eric had been standing beside her when he, too, sat down on the pier. He didn't say anything. Not for a long time. Then he murmured, "I always end up apologizing to you." When she didn't respond, he continued, "None of this is your fault. I don't blame you for asking David to show you around. And I don't really blame him for doing it. I would have, too, given the same set of circumstances."

"Why didn't you tell him that?" she asked huskily.

Eric ran a hand through his hair and sighed. "David and I can't seem to admit things like that to each other anymore."

"You could once?" she asked.

He nodded. "A long, long time ago, yes." He seemed to lose himself in time. When he shook free, he glanced at her and asked, "Tell me, how are you settling in? Have you enjoyed your first week at Heron's Inn, or have you had your fill of us Marshalls?"

Robin let herself smile. She was still upset, but if he was prepared to make an effort, she could, too. "I like it here," she replied slowly.

"You aren't lonely?"

"How could I be?"

"Some people think the peace and quiet go too far."

"But it's so beautiful!"

"Some people can't see that." She looked at him curiously. "Are we speaking of Da-

73

vid, by any chance?"

He leaned back, propping himself on his outstretched hands. "Yes," he said, then added, "He seems to like you."

"Is that so surprising?"

"He doesn't like many people, that's all."

"I wouldn't say he *likes* me. We only talked for a few minutes."

"If he talked to you for any length of time at all, that's something. Believe me."

"What about his friends?"

Eric shook his head. "He doesn't have any friends."

"But —"

"Oh, maybe one or two that he calls friends. But I've never seen them. I'm not sure they even exist."

Robin frowned. "Doesn't that worry you?" she asked slowly.

"Worries the hell out of me! But what can I do?"

"Maybe you could try not being so hard on him."

"You think I'm too hard on him?"

"Well, yes, in a way."

"And you base this theory on one week's observation?"

Robin started to rock again, her gaze refocusing on the water. She couldn't admit that she knew their past history far better than he thought she did, that she felt an almost spiritual connection with the family. "It was merely a suggestion," she murmured.

Long, capable fingers reached out to draw her chin around. Her internal alarm system jerked to a higher stage of alert and she stopped rocking. Her gaze fluttered to his and then away again.

"What *is* it about you?" he asked softly a moment later. He sounded genuinely puzzled.

Robin moved her chin away. "I don't know what you mean."

He made no reply, and when she chanced another glance at him, it was to see that he was frowning.

Her heart was thumping rapidly, and her breathing had turned shallow. She tried to tell herself she was reacting to the possibility that he suspected who she was, but that idea was inconceivable. There was no possible way he might suspect.

She scrambled to her feet. "I think . . . I think I'll go for a walk."

He stood up, as well. "We have several good hiking trails in the area."

"I think I'll follow the cliff."

"If you continue that way for about half a mile, you'll come to a fork where the path branches off to the beach. If you go straight, you'll eventually come to the Overlook. It's a favorite place for whale watchers in winter and spring. Unfortunately, the migration is over right now. All you'll have is a great view."

"Great."

"It's about five miles," he warned.

"I'll decide what I want to do when I get to the fork."

Eric knew very clearly what he wanted to do — follow her, take her hand, walk with her, *be* with her — and the force of the impulse shocked him. It didn't subside until Robin had reached the headland and turned to walk along the cliff path. And even then he had a hard time calling himself to order. He'd done his best to stay away from her all week, hoping that if he avoided the problem it might cease to exist. Only his plan hadn't worked. He would have had to move out of the house not to run into her, and adopting a formal manner only made him feel foolish. Several times he'd caught Samantha looking at him strangely. The last thing he needed was for her to catch on.

Robin didn't want to walk. She wanted to get in her car and drive back to her apartment in the Berkeley hills. She wanted familiar things around her. She wanted to see her friends.

The drive to the Bay Area and back was too long and too difficult to make easily in one day, though. A narrow, twisting road following the coastline or a narrow, twisting road through dense forests before she could finally break out onto the Interstate. It was possible to accomplish, but tomorrow she would be a wreck.

She followed the pathway, trying not to think. And when she came to the fork in the road, she chose the branch that led to the beach. The descent was easier than she expected, fairly level in places, with a series of steps built into the steeper areas.

The waves off the open ocean struck the shore with much more violence than in the protected cove, smashing against the tumbled rocks. Driftwood was scattered along the narrow beach's tide line, along with bits and pieces of seaweed. Sea gulls patrolled for food on foot and in the air.

The wind whipped at her clothes and hair while the sun remained hidden behind the bluff. She might have been alone in all the world, except for the several sets of footprints dotting the firm sand, evidence that someone had traveled this way before.

Nearly washed away in some spots, the prints remained true to form in others. Robin wondered if the people had walked singly or in a group. Next, she wondered who they might be. Then part of her question was answered.

Barbara Marshall stood just around a turn of the shoreline, as still as a statue, staring out to sea. Robin instantly halted, reluctant to disturb her, but Barbara had already sensed another presence. She broke into a smile as she greeted Robin warmly.

"Isn't it a beautiful morning?" she asked pleasantly. "I love the air out here. It's so clean and clear." She filled her lungs and blissfully exhaled. "I'm going to miss it when Timothy and I go to live in Sacramento."

"Sacramento?" Robin echoed. "I didn't realize —"

Barbara smiled wryly. "Me, neither. When we got engaged, I had no idea. But Timothy's been offered a job in the office of our local state representative, and we can't afford to turn it down." She grinned. "His mother isn't sure whether to brag or to cry. Timothy thinks that getting away for the first few years of our marriage is a good idea. I agree with him. His mother's a dear, but she does like to run things."

"Sacramento isn't that far away."

"Just far enough!" Barbara quipped, and both women laughed. They fell into step to walk along the beach.

"When exactly is the wedding?" Robin asked.

"It's scheduled for June 20th."

Robin sensed an underlying concern in Barbara's voice. "That sounds a little tentative," she responded.

"At the rate we're going, Eileen — she's Timothy's mother — isn't going to have any hair left by the day of the wedding! She keeps tearing it out, strand by strand, because we keep having one problem after another."

"Is she trying to do too much?"

"Yes. But every time I try to help, she insists on doing it her way." Barbara sighed. "I don't want to create tension between us. As I said before, she's a dear. But —"

"But it is your wedding."

"And Timothy's. Only he's beginning to disappear the minute anyone mentions the word."

"Which irritates you."

"It's starting to!"

Robin smiled. "You have, what — three weeks left? It will all be over soon."

"I hope so. But some of the plans are

beginning to look shaky. Eileen says not to worry, but I find it hard not to."

"If there's anything I can do . . ." Robin offered.

Barbara looked at her. "You know, you've only been here for a week, but it seems much longer. Before you came, things were pretty rough. I had to be away so often. Eileen insists that I come to every appointment, even though she does most of the talking. Eric and Samantha were wearing themselves out at the inn, doing all of their work plus mine. I suppose, to be fair, I should include David, but most times it's easier to do the job yourself than to oversee him. Since you've been here, though, I don't feel quite so guilty."

Robin nodded understanding.

"You've also fit right in emotionally, if you know what I mean," Barbara continued. "It's as if you're some sort of kindred spirit!"

Robin shrugged uneasily. "It hasn't been that hard."

"Eric is very pleased with your work," Barbara confided. "He hasn't said much, but I can tell."

They proceeded in silence another few minutes before deciding to turn back. Robin stooped to pick up an interesting shell, moving it this way and that in the bright sunlight.

"I once had a huge collection of shells," Barbara remarked. "I was eighteen when we moved here from San Francisco. Actually, that's how I met Timothy. We were both on the beach, walking from different directions, him from Vista Point — that's the old lumber mill town where he lives about ten miles up the coast — and me from Dunnigan Bay. We were both looking for shells. We met, and we fell in love at the exact same instant. Isn't that romantic?"

"Almost as if it were preordained," Robin remarked.

"I believe some things are."

"Both good and bad?" Robin asked, her thoughts automatically turning to the accident.

Barbara frowned. "I suppose so, yes."

Had their father's death been preordained? Robin wondered. It would be such a relief to believe that. But it also seemed too easy a way out, an excuse to cling to when reality became too hard to take. Robin concentrated on the present. "Why did your family move to Dunnigan Bay?" she asked. It seemed as good a time as any to ask, and Barbara the right person.

Barbara glanced at Robin, as though try-

81

ing to gauge how much she could tell her. "Because of David," she said finally. "He was having all kinds of trouble in school and in the neighborhood where we lived. He was getting into fights. He was only ten, but he was picking on boys that were fifteen and sixteen. You can imagine the result. Eric tried everything he could to fix the situation. Nothing worked. David couldn't get along with the kids his age, either, and the authorities at the school had had enough. They were about to transfer him to a special teaching facility. Eric thought a move might help — take David out of the city, away from the people he got into trouble with, away from the teachers who'd given up on him. So we came here."

"How did the rest of you feel about that? Did you mind moving?"

"We all wanted to help David."

Robin hesitated. "It didn't do very much good, though, did it?"

Barbara shook her head sadly. "No. He just transferred his anger to Eric. I don't know why."

"Has he had any kind of professional help?"

"A score of school psychologists. Sometimes I think they made things worse. They certainly didn't help him."

"No one since that time?"

"David would never agree to go! Can you imagine if one of us suggested such a thing? He'd bite our heads off."

"How did it turn out that Eric was in charge? I mean . . . what happened to your parents?"

There. It was out. She had to be told formally, otherwise they'd wonder why she hadn't asked.

"Oh! You don't know about that, do you? Our father was killed sixteen years ago — sixteen years last month, as a matter of fact — when he rescued a young girl from drowning. She survived but he didn't. She was just a couple of years older than me."

Robin's hand had unconsciously tightened on the shell, causing its rough edges to cut her skin.

"He was considered a hero," Barbara continued. "We even made a trip to Washington, D.C., to receive a medal given posthum— pos—" She had trouble with the word. "One presented after his death. It was in all the newspapers and on TV." Her voice caught. "It still hurts," she said by way of explanation.

"What happened to the girl?" Robin was compelled to ask.

"I don't know. We never met her."

"And your mother?"

"Our mother died shortly after David was born. An aneurysm in the brain. No one suspected. One day she was with us, the next she wasn't. The same as our dad."

"Oh, my God," Robin breathed, stunned.

"Eric didn't have much of a choice. If we were to stay together as a family, he had to leave college to take care of us. We had an aunt and uncle who lived in another state, but they weren't in a position to take the five of us who were underage. So Eric quit his senior year, and he never went back."

"He never married, either?" Robin asked. It was important for her to hear that he had. That he had had someone to help ease the circumstances.

"Never," Barbara said softly.

Robin could think of nothing else to say. She had already learned more than she could absorb for the moment.

Shortly afterward, they arrived at the trail that led back to the ridge. Barbara took it, while Robin continued to walk along the beach.

This time, no footprints marked the sand ahead of her. She was truly alone.

CHAPTER FIVE

"A letter from Bridget!" Samantha cried, waving an envelope in the air. "I get to read it first!" She curled into a Windsor chair beside the small table in the kitchen. The table was placed a short distance from the French doors opening into the garden.

Eric came out of the utility room carrying freshly filled spray bottles of cleanser. "Has she found her cousin, the earl, yet?" he teased.

"I don't know." Samantha busily scanned the cramped writing. She giggled. "She says she kissed the Blarney stone and almost put her back out because you have to do it lying on your back and with your head hanging down."

"She doesn't need any more blarney," Eric grumbled.

"Wait! Wait! She does say something about the earl . . ." Samantha became engrossed in what she was reading and forgot to relate

85

it to the others.

Eric grinned at Robin. "She does this to keep up the tension."

Robin glanced fondly at Samantha. The girl continued to be a delight. Part woman, part child, she brightened each day with her sunny personality and hopeful outlook on life. Few things seemed to worry her.

Robin turned back to see that Eric had not looked away from her. She concentrated on cutting the vegetables for the potpies scheduled for that evening's meal.

When Eric left the room, Robin breathed an unconscious sigh of relief.

"I think Timothy's mother better start worrying," Samantha observed wryly. "Things are starting to look pretty interesting around here."

"What are you talking about?" Robin questioned, even though she already had a good idea.

"You and Eric."

"There is no 'me and Eric.' "

"That's not what I saw from over here."

"I thought you were reading your letter."

"I was."

"Then —"

"I finished it."

"There *is* no me and Eric," Robin repeated.

86

"Uh-huh." It was obvious Samantha didn't believe her, and Robin flashed the girl an irritated look.

Samantha uncoiled from the chair. "I don't suppose it's very smart of me to annoy the cook when she's wielding a knife."

"Don't you have some windows to clean or something?" Robin muttered.

"Mirrors," Samantha corrected her. "I have to clean the mirrors."

Robin lifted an eyebrow and tapped her foot. It was a signal the line chefs in the kitchen of Le Jardin knew well.

Samantha snapped a mock salute and disappeared into the utility room. A minute later she marched out, glass-cleaning equipment in hand, along with a feather duster which she'd propped over her left shoulder.

Robin started to chuckle, only to turn serious again when her thoughts returned to Eric Marshall. With no one watching, she took her frustration out on the vegetables, making quick work of the remainder of the celery, carrots and onions. In a few seconds she was done.

"Wow!" David said admiringly from the kitchen doorway.

Robin's head jerked up. She'd thought he was down the street with his French tutor!

He stepped into the room, an awed smile

still tilting his lips. "I didn't know anyone could cut like that! How did you do it?"

In the two weeks Robin had been at Heron's Inn, she had worked diligently to keep her secret. She tried to make light of the situation. "I didn't do anything special."

"Do it again," he urged her.

Robin collected the cut vegetables into several plastic refrigerator containers. "I have all I need."

"Aw, come on. Please?"

"I don't like to waste food."

He flipped the top from the celery container and reached inside. "Just like one of those machines," he murmured, letting the uniform slices slip between his fingers.

"You should wash your hands before you handle food," Robin chastised. She pulled the box away and stored it on a refrigerator shelf.

"Don't get all bent out of shape," David said as he leaned against the counter. "I came to ask if you'd like to go for a bike ride."

"You mean now?" she asked, surprised.

His rare smile was just like Eric's. That same flash of easy charm. "I didn't mean tomorrow."

"I can't now," she answered. "I have to make dinner."

"Dinner can wait."

"No, it can't."

"You're the cook. Dinner is when *you* say it is."

"That's right. I am the cook. I have certain responsi—"

"You're beginning to sound like Eric!" he interrupted sharply. "Am I going to have to start calling you Saint Robin?"

"That's entirely up to you," she said levelly. "Any other time, David, I'd love to come. But right now I can't. Please try and understand."

He continued to look at her, a mixture of emotions passing through his blue eyes. The sentiment he settled on was aggrieved petulance. "If you don't want to go, just say so. I have other things I can do, and other people I can do them with."

Robin wondered if she was cutting off all future contact with the boy, but she stood her ground. "That's not what I said. But if that's the way you feel, go ahead."

"I will." David ground the words out. He pushed away from the counter and disappeared into the hall. Seconds later, the front door slammed shut.

Robin's frustration mounted. She'd wanted to grow closer to David, to help him if she could. So what did she end up doing?

Send him off in a huff the first time he made a substantial move toward friendship. But at least he *had* reached out. She could only hope that he would do it again.

At the edge of her field of vision, a subtle movement caught Robin's attention. She turned, wondering if David had come back. But David wasn't there. Neither was anyone else. She frowned, fruitlessly searching the area again. She would have sworn . . .

Goose bumps lifted the hair on her forearms and at the back of her neck. A ghost? She swallowed remembering the shadows Eric told her Bridget had seen. She tried to convince herself that she was mistaken. She hadn't seen anything. But if nothing was there, if nothing had moved, what had drawn her attention?

She reached out to the counter for support. And it was at that moment Eric strode into the room.

She was pale and looked as if her legs no longer wanted to support her. Eric hurried to her side.

Placing a protective arm around her shoulders, he demanded, "What happened? I heard the front door slam. What did David say? What did he do?"

"It wasn't David," she replied shakily. She

drew away from him and cleared her throat. "I thought I saw — nothing. I saw nothing. I'm perfectly all right."

"You don't look perfectly all right to me."

"I am! I just —"

"Come on," he urged her. "Sit down before I have to peel you off the floor."

She allowed him to assist her into the same chair Samantha had used earlier. He waited for her to collect herself. When he sensed that his looming height was uncomfortable to her, he hunkered down on one knee so that their heads would be nearer the same level.

He examined her closely. Something had unnerved her, and he didn't fully believe the cause not to be David. "Would you like something to drink?" he asked.

She shook her head.

"Water," he explained, unsure if she had understood his offer.

Once again she shook her head. Her brown eyes avoided his.

He brushed a strand of hair away from her face. It was an intimate act that he tried to tell himself was merely solicitous. Still, it released a tumultuous array of emotions inside him. It had been a long time since he'd touched a woman with any feeling of sensuousness. He drew a steadying breath.

"I'm fine . . . really," she claimed. "I have to finish cooking dinner."

When she attempted to stand, he stopped her. "Just stay put for a few minutes. There's no rush about anything."

"But I have to have dinner ready on time."

"Who's the boss around here?" he demanded with a touch of humor.

"I thought I was — in the kitchen."

"Most times, yes. At this moment, no. We can't have you reporting us to the Labor Relations Board as bad employers."

"I wouldn't do that."

"Or picketing the place."

"I wouldn't do that, either." A little of her normal color had returned under his good-natured teasing.

"Or writing to Bridget that I've been a bad boss. My life would be hell when she got back."

"You aren't afraid of Bridget, are you?"

"I'm terrified!"

She laughed, but she gave an uneasy glance over her shoulder.

After a moment, he prompted her softly. "Would you like to tell me what happened?"

"I think . . . I may have seen your ghost," she admitted.

His first reaction was to say "You're kidding!" But he held back because of the way she'd looked when he first entered the room.

She hadn't been pretending. Instead, he said, "We don't have any ghosts here, remember?"

"Then your *shadow*. I saw something. At least, I sort of did. It was . . . over there." She motioned in the direction of the stove. "I know this sounds crazy. I'd think that myself if I hadn't seen it. Except . . . I'm sure I saw something move. Just out of the line of my vision." She hesitated. "You've never seen it?"

He shook his head. "Never."

She sighed and looked away from him.

Eric found himself wanting to reclaim her gaze. "But just because I've never seen it . . ." He let the sentence trail off, offering another possibility.

Her warm brown eyes returned to his. He'd never seen eyes that same color. Not in his entire life. And they were set in a face that had started to haunt his every waking moment and even some of his dreams. She watched him solemnly, testing the truth of his resolve. His gaze slid to her lips. They were soft and perfectly curved.

"Thank you for not laughing at me," she said at last.

Eric nodded slowly. He appreciated that she appreciated his attitude. But at that moment, it wasn't the most important thing on his mind. He was driven by a need to taste those lips, to experience their warmth, to feel them as they moved beneath his. He couldn't look away. Then he leaned forward, drawn by an inevitability he could no longer resist.

"Robin," he breathed. It might have been a question, it might not. She sat perfectly still.

Honey . . . warm, melting honey. Her lips had an addicting sweetness that offered no cure except more of the same. A thousand tiny wildfires burst into life in his veins.

When he pulled back, she looked as stunned as he felt, as caught up in the moment. She didn't seem displeased.

He leaned forward to kiss her again, only this time he didn't plan on pulling away so soon.

She blinked and jerked away from the table, escaping his reach. "Why did you do that?" she demanded, suddenly angry.

He stood up, doing his best to call himself to order. "Because I felt like it."

"I wish you hadn't!"

His senses continued to swim. The imprint of her mouth still burned on his. "I've wanted to do that for at least a week," he admitted.

She whirled around, presenting him with her back.

If she hoped to discourage him, it didn't work. He enjoyed every view of her, the graceful curve of spine and hips, the length of slender thigh.

"Well, don't do it again," she ordered.

"That's not the way it works. Are you telling me you didn't enjoy it?"

"Yes!"

"Liar," he said softly.

She moved jerkily to the counter and measured out flour and salt into a wide bowl. She then busied herself at the refrigerator, standing in front of the open door. When finally she closed it, her cheeks were a lighter shade of pink.

Once he realized what she'd done, he smiled. She'd stood in front of the open refrigerator to cool off! If anything could help him regain his equilibrium, it was that. His smile grew into an amused chuckle.

"What are you laughing at?" she demanded irritably.

The front door of the house shut loudly, saving him from having to find an answer. Seconds later, Barbara burst into the room, too wrapped up in her own troubles to suspect that she might be interrupting anything between Eric and Robin.

95

"Everything's ruined!" she wailed dramatically. "The reception, the wedding . . . everything!" Then she threw herself onto that morning's well-used chair and burst into a torrent of tears.

Robin watched as Eric switched from romantic hero to father figure. His focus immediately changed. He brought the matching Windsor chair around the table so that he could sit close to his sister and pulled her into his embrace. It was as if in his arms she could be protected against all the ills of the world. She gratefully accepted his solace, burying her face in his shoulder while curling her fingers into his shirt. He stroked her thick hair, making occasional soft sounds of sympathy.

Robin forgot the piecrust she had started. She forgot her flare of anger. She remembered her own father holding her in a similar way, whether to console her because a beloved pet had died or because someone she thought to be a friend had been unkind. She hadn't had such comforting since she was eighteen, since shortly before her father's death. For a moment her body ached to be held by him again in that very special way.

Barbara tried to regain control. She sat back from her brother's embrace and rubbed at her wet eyes and cheeks. When Eric offered her a tissue, she blew her nose.

"What's happened?" Eric asked quietly.

"I'm sorry," Barbara whispered. Her gaze flitted to Robin and away again, embarrassed. "I didn't mean to cause such a scene. It's just — I held it in while I was with Timothy and Eileen. She was about to go through the roof. You'll probably get a call. I'm truly beginning to worry about her. But she won't hear of scaling things down. And now the people she hired to make the cakes have gone out of business! One of her friends called this morning to tell her the bad news. We rushed over and the place was shut tight." Tears again welled in her eyes. "There was a Gone Out Of Business sign and no one will answer the phone. Eileen even called the police, but it didn't do any good. The people have just picked up and left. With our deposit, with our cakes . . . or what would have been our cakes." Tears again rolled over Barbara's splotched cheeks until they became a stream.

Robin edged closer. Eric glanced at her and then back at his sister. She saw nothing in his eyes to indicate that he recalled what had passed between them such a short time before.

"Can't you call someone else?" he suggested.

"On such short notice? No. There's only one other bakery Eileen will even consider and they're all booked up. It's June. Lots of people get married in June. She offered them double the money, but —" She swallowed. "I tried to get her to ask someone in Vista Point but she doesn't want to do it. I ended up yelling at her. It was awful!" she wailed. "I was trying to be so careful. Timothy looked at me as if I'd suddenly grown two heads. But I just couldn't take it anymore! Now I'm not sure if there's even going to *be* a wedding. I tried to apologize, but she's so determined that the wedding be perfect." Barbara's shoulders started to shake and she hid her face in her hands.

Samantha had come to stand in the doorway. "I heard," she said softly.

Robin cleared her throat. "Uh . . . possibly I can help."

Everyone looked at her.

"I — I spent some time working in a bakery," she continued. "I could make the wedding cakes."

Her claim was met with silence.

She shifted under their stares. "I could make a test cake, if you like, to give you a sample."

"You'd do that?" Barbara asked, traces of tears still glistening on her cheeks.

Robin nodded.

Hope brightened Barbara's expression. "We'd pay you," she assured her.

Robin declined. "If you agree — if Eileen agrees — we'll make it my present to you and Timothy. I know I haven't been here very long, but —"

Barbara jumped up to give her a quick hug, and Samantha hurried over to join them. Robin met Eric's gaze. His pale eyes smiled in appreciation.

The telephone rang. Samantha ran to get it. "It's Timothy," she called a few seconds later. Barbara made a trilling sound and rushed away.

Left alone with Robin, Eric said, "Thank you."

Robin shrugged. "I couldn't stand by and let the wedding fall apart."

"You're a woman of many hidden talents."

Samantha popped back into the room. "I hate to interrupt," she said, "but the Whittakers have arrived and would like to be shown to their room. He seems a bit out of sorts."

"He's always out of sorts," Eric said. "Don't you remember him from last year? I was surprised when he booked again, after all his complaints."

"Which room are you giving them? I could show them up," Samantha offered.

"The large suite in front."

"The one with the oversize tub for two?" She grinned. "Somehow he doesn't look the romantic sort."

"It's what he requested," Eric said.

A few seconds later, a voice raised in protest could be heard coming from the entry hall. "My wife and I want a meal now! We haven't eaten since we left home. I don't care if this place doesn't normally serve lunch. Surely you have some bread and some cheese or something. It can't be all that difficult to produce."

Eric sighed. "I should have told him we were full up," he muttered.

"I can make something if you like," Robin offered.

"Don't go to too much trouble."

"Sandwiches, just as the man said."

He started to walk away but stopped. "Do you think you could find some extremely old cheese? The moldier the better."

"I'll look," Robin promised.

A few moments later she heard him in the hall, sorting out the difficulty. Then several sets of feet tramped upstairs to the second floor.

When Eric returned to the kitchen sooner than she expected — Samantha must have taken the new arrivals upstairs as she'd offered — he grinned, enjoying her surprise.

"I was kidding about the cheese, of course," he said easily.

Robin made her eyes very wide. "You were? But I thought —" She motioned to the sandwich she had partially constructed.

"Surely you didn't take me at my word," he said tightly as he hurried across the room.

He pulled away the lettuce and tomato to expose the cheese below. The thin slices were beautiful examples of their type, a pale, creamy Swiss. Not one spot of mold marred their hole-filled perfection.

"Another of my *many* talents," she quipped softly.

An appreciative smile tugged at his lips. For the moment, he conceded, she had bested him.

CHAPTER SIX

An unusually heavy fog enshrouded Dunnigan Bay and the surrounding coast for most of the next day, and the guests registered at the inn stayed close by. Most of them caused little extra work. They seemed to be enjoying a day spent relaxing around the toasty-warm fire crackling in the living room fireplace, reading books, playing games and engaging one another and the Marshalls in conversation. The Whittakers were the exception.

There were no televisions for the guests' use and the only telephones in the large house were the one in the family quarters on the top floor and the one installed in a shallow niche under the main stairway. Cell service was all but nonexistent. Normally, the guests reveled in getting away from the frantic pace of modern life. Frank Whittaker acted as if such inconveniences were directed specifically against him.

"What kind of place is this?" he demanded of anyone who would listen. "What do you mean, you don't have a big-screen TV? I thought you had one right over there last year." He jabbed a finger toward the far corner of the living room. "What did you do with it? Why don't you bring it back out? I don't care if it's too foggy, I'm going to walk to the Overlook! If I can't watch TV and I can't have a private telephone conversation and you recommend I not walk to the Overlook, then why am I here? Pack our bags, Alma! We're going home!"

Alma took her husband's rantings meekly, but she made no effort to pack their bags and he didn't truly seem to expect her to. Frank Whittaker was the kind of person who liked to hear himself talk — the louder the better. He seldom followed through with any of his threats. At least, that was the conclusion Robin came to after being forced to listen to him for most of the day. She was amazed that there hadn't been an uprising, with the other guests tossing him over the cliff.

After dinner, when her nerves seemed stretched to their limit, he went to sleep in one of the wing chairs in the living room and started a quiet, rhythmic snoring.

Eric was engrossed in a game of cribbage

with Donal Caldwell, who, as usual, planned to spend the entire summer at Heron's Inn. Samantha was upstairs in the family quarters, and Barbara, her wedding back on schedule, was out with Timothy.

Robin had originally planned to use her free time that evening to start making the decorative sugar flowers for the test cake, but she just didn't feel up to it. It was intricate work, requiring a much steadier hand than she had at the moment. Instead, once the kitchen was secured for the night, Robin made her way upstairs.

The third floor of the house had been cleverly converted from what might have been depressingly small rooms in which servants did little else than sleep to a warm and friendly place in which the family could relax and socialize. The bedrooms remained small, but the ones that Robin had seen were comfortable. The long room at the front of the house, now used as the family's common room, had been created from two smaller rooms.

Samantha was curled into her favorite place on the camel-colored couch, an oversize book spread open in her lap. With her long legs tucked beneath her, she absently twisted a curling length of blond hair. She looked up when Robin came into the room.

"Has Eric told the Whittakers to leave yet?" she asked.

"Not that I know of."

"Too bad."

"How long are they going to stay?" Robin asked.

Samantha made a face. "Until the weekend. I don't know if I can stand it if this fog doesn't clear. Morning and evening fog in summer, that's typical here. But not like this, where everyone has to listen to Frank Whittaker complain all the time."

Robin settled on the couch. At times, she still had difficulty making herself mingle freely with the Marshalls. She couldn't forget who she was, who they were.

"Would you like to read Bridget's letter?" Samantha asked, surprising her.

"Certainly," Robin agreed.

The letter was full of what the older woman had seen and done, and her excitement concerning a story she'd heard about the English earl she was trying to trace. It seemed the earl truly did exist and spent most of his time at his house in London. On rare occasions, though, he returned to his ancestral home in County Cork, which had been constructed adjacent to the crumbling fortlike castle that members of his family had owned since the late twelfth century. Bridget felt she was related to him on his mother's side, his Irish side. Her excitement sprang from the fact that he was rumored to be planning a visit before the summer was out. She closed her letter with admonitions to the family to take proper care of themselves and with a question as to how her substitute was working out.

Robin smiled at the doubt evident in the question. Bridget didn't think anyone capable of properly filling her position with the family, and if it wasn't for the possibility that the earl might come, she would probably cut short her trip and return immediately.

"She's quite a character," Robin murmured.

Samantha thrust the photo album she was holding toward her. "This is Bridget," she said, pointing to a tiny woman with a round face, white hair and a determined expression. "She's really much more of a marshmallow than she looks. I hope she gets to meet her earl. It will mean so much to her."

"She mentions Barbara's wedding in the letter," Robin said. "How is it that she's in Ireland when the wedding is so close?"

Samantha found a more comfortable position for her folded legs, though she kept them beneath her. "That was a *huge* problem. The trip was set for earlier in the spring, but Maureen — that's Bridget's traveling companion — broke her leg, so it had to be postponed. The only time Maureen could go was summer — she's accepted a teaching position in the fall. So Bridget was forced into it, if she wanted to go at all. We practically ordered her to go, because she'd been planning the trip for so long. Years, actually. She didn't want to at first, but Barbara promised to film the wedding so she wouldn't miss any of it."

Robin studied the other photos on the page. There were recent pictures of Barbara and Samantha and others she knew must be Benjamin, Allison, and Allison's two children.

"That's our sister Allison," Samantha confirmed, pointing her out. "And the twins, Colin and Gwen . . . they're ten. That's Benjamin, our other brother." She encouraged Robin to look through the book. "Our Disneyland trip. The Grand Canyon. Yellowstone. We went to Yellowstone with our mom and dad. See? That's our mother. And that's our dad."

Robin's stomach twisted sharply. Martin Marshall. Not in the business suit and studio pose she was familiar with from her newspaper clippings. Not with his silver blond hair plastered wetly to his head, a look of forced good cheer in his pale blue eyes as he fought for their lives. Not lying on the beach, unmoving. In this picture he was with his family, relaxing in tan shorts and a blue-and-white striped polo shirt, frozen in time as he laughed with his pregnant wife and four of his five children. Eric wasn't in the photograph. Robin wondered numbly if he had taken the picture.

She stared at Martin Marshall for a long time before allowing her gaze to move on to his wife. Like her husband, she was tall and blonde, and they even had a similar look. No wonder their children so resembled one another. She must have been pregnant with David. About seven months, Robin guessed. She was smiling broadly at the camera, while one child — Samantha — clung tightly to her leg.

They looked so alive! So happy!

"I was three when that picture was taken. To tell you the truth," Samantha admitted, "I don't remember it. I don't remember very much about my mother, either. I remember when she died, but not . . . her." She sighed sadly. "I remember a little more about my dad." She looked expectantly at Robin. "Has anyone told you about our dad?"

Robin nodded. She couldn't speak.

"I was five years old when he died," Samantha continued. "I remember he'd promised to take us to the park. I was just getting over the chicken pox and the lady who was taking care of us then had left. I didn't like her. All she did all day was sit and watch TV and tell us to be quiet. Eric came home early from college and found her asleep while Benjamin and David and I were in the kitchen trying to make lunch. Eric told Dad, and Dad dismissed her. Anyway, Dad thought we needed a treat that day. I was still a bit scabby from the chicken pox, but Dad didn't care. He said I looked like I was wearing a polka-dot body suit! Allison helped us get ready and we waited. And waited. It was a Saturday, but Dad had to meet a man for an appointment before we could leave. He never came home."

Robin pushed the book away and stood up. She couldn't look at it anymore. Nor could she continue to listen. She knew what had happened. *She* had happened.

Samantha struggled to her feet. "Oh! I didn't mean to upset you! It's okay. Really, it is. It's been so long. We've all . . . adjusted. It was bad for a while, but Eric took over and made things right for us again. Our dad was a hero. He saved someone's *life*. That's something to be extremely proud of, Bridget says. She thinks Eric is wrong to blame the girl. It wasn't her fault."

Eric blamed the girl. Robin felt her stomach lurch. What would he do if he was to find out . . .

"What are you two doing?" Eric asked from across the room.

Both women jumped.

"We were just — I was showing —" For the first time since Robin had known her, Samantha was at a loss for words. She didn't seem to want Eric to know what they'd been talking about.

"Samantha was showing me your photo album," Robin said, filling the silence. For her own reasons, she didn't want him to know what they'd been discussing, either.

"Which one?" Eric asked. He came across the room, picked up the discarded album and started to thumb through it. "At least it's not the one with all our baby pictures. Mom had a penchant for bare bottoms and sheepskin rugs. She even managed to get one of David before —" His words broke off, but the unsaid thought hung in the air.

"It's blackmail," Robin inserted with forced cheerfulness. "Parents use them for blackmail. Mine's not on a sheepskin rug. I'm skinny-dipping in my blow-up pool."

"How old were you?" Eric asked, a twinkle in his eye.

"Five. I was a water sprite with flowers in my hair."

"I'd like to see it," he teased softly.

"No way!" she teased back.

Samantha pulled the photo album from her brother's grasp and returned it to the nearby bookcase. "I think I'll go to my room now. I have a letter to write . . . to Bridget."

Eric's gaze didn't waver from Robin. "Tell her I'll write to her soon," he said.

A knowing smile tilted Samantha's lips as she looked from one to the other. "So if you two will excuse me . . ."

"Scat!" Eric ordered when, after a moment, she still hadn't left.

Samantha giggled, then did as he said.

Robin moved uneasily about the room. She couldn't stay still after what she'd just heard . . . and seen . . . and learned. Possibly her parents and Dr. Mays had known what they were talking about when they advised against her meeting the Marshalls all those years ago. Possibly there were some things a person just shouldn't do — ever.

Eric sat down on the couch. Nothing she did escaped his notice. Robin knew she should excuse herself, as well, but she couldn't make herself do it. He was like a flame, and she the moth. She continued to dance around him.

He blamed her. He blamed her. The words replayed themselves in her mind. But he didn't know it was her!

"Why don't you ease up a bit?" he suggested. "It's been a hard day. I had to restrain myself to keep from telling Frank Whittaker to take that little hike in the fog he wanted so badly. There are at least three places along the trail to the Overlook where he could fall off. Maybe he'd have found one."

"I can't imagine being married to him."

"He's a lucky man."

Robin frowned. "Why's that?"

"Because he *isn't* married to you. I saw the way you looked at him when he complained about dinner."

"That was only because he'd already complained about his dinner last night, and his breakfast and lunch today. He even said his sandwich yesterday tasted funny."

"If he only knew," Eric murmured.

"I *should* have found some moldy cheese."

Eric laughed and patted the cushion at his side. "Come on. Sit down." Then he added softly, "I promise I won't bite."

"I'm fine where I am, thanks."

"I'll get a crick in my neck trying to see

you back there."

She had stopped behind the couch to finger a pale pink rose petal that had dropped onto the table from the small bouquet, one of many scattered freely throughout the inn.

"Then don't look," she retorted, and had to look away herself because he was so attractive with his head leaning back against the camel-colored couch, the natural unruliness of his thick blond hair just begging her to trail her fingers through it, his blue eyes half-closed in lazy estimation.

"You aren't, are you?" he asked.

"Aren't what?"

"Married."

She laughed shortly. "No!"

"Don't you expect to be . . . one day?"

Robin moved away from the couch to a window. She parted the curtains to look outside, but she saw nothing, not even the fog. Her concentration was focused solely on this room. "What about you?" she asked instead.

"You didn't answer my question."

"And you didn't answer mine."

He sat forward, his elbows on his knees. "No, I'm not married."

"Ever expect to be?"

His gaze was quizzical. "That's a fairly

113

personal question."

"It's what you asked me."

"You laughed," he accused her. "You made me curious."

"So am I . . . curious."

He stood up and came to the window, stopping directly across from her. He didn't pretend that his interest was in the view. Instead, his hand came out to cover her cheek, his fingertips spreading into her hair, touching the sensitive curve of her ear. "Why?" he asked softly. "Why are you curious? I know my reason. Do you know yours?"

She had been close to him before. Yesterday, when he'd kissed her. But yesterday had been unexpected. Was this unexpected, too? Or had she wanted it to happen, waited for it?

"Don't," she breathed, unable to raise her voice above a whisper. She felt as if every nerve in her body was stretched in anticipation. She was aware of him — of the warmth emanating from his long, lean body, the power behind his gentleness, the promise of what might happen if she allowed the moment to play itself out.

"Why not?" he murmured huskily. He shifted closer.

Robin's senses reeled. She had to break

this off. He blamed her — her! — for all the troubles that had befallen his family. She couldn't let . . . An overpowering thought suddenly occurred to her. She could ignore everything. He didn't know who she was, and he might never find out. Not if she didn't tell him.

His arms encircled her. His lips took the place of his hand on her cheek, before moving on to the sensitive skin of her neck, of her ear, then finally to her mouth.

Long, conflicting moments later she broke contact. "No . . . no . . . I can't!" she cried raggedly, gasping for air. "I — I can't!" She tried to push him away.

At first he didn't move, then eventually he set her free. She rocked unsteadily on her feet.

"You can't say you didn't enjoy that," he challenged unevenly.

Her gaze slid away. "I — I —" She felt him watching her, waiting for her to express a coherent thought. "I make it a habit never to get involved with — with anyone at my place of employment, especially my employer," she finally managed.

He absorbed what she'd said, then countered with, "Has this been a recurring problem?"

"No."

"Not that I would doubt it," he added quickly. "A woman as appealing as you would —"

"Let's just forget it, okay?" she interrupted him, desperately wanting the moment to be over.

A self-deprecating smile touched his lips as he shrugged lightly. "That's the trouble. I don't think I can forget it."

Robin reminded herself of the need to resist his charm.

"We've already taken the first step," he continued.

She shook her head. "No, we haven't."

His slow smile spread. "If you insist."

"Stop it!"

"Stop what?"

"Stop mocking me."

"I have three sisters, remember? I know when a woman is covering her tracks."

"You think you know so much."

"If I do, I've learned it the hard way. Raising three girls isn't the easiest thing in the world for a man on his own. A young man. One who isn't sure about anything!" He paused, shifting away from his brief flare-up of anger. "Barbara told me she explained about our father."

Robin's nerves tightened. "Yes," she replied, moving back behind the couch. For something to do, she collected the fallen rose petals. She didn't want to talk about it. Not now. Not with him. She'd already been through enough. But she couldn't make herself leave.

"It was a *stupid* thing to have happened," he said tightly. "Such a waste. He was only forty-one. Four years older than I am now." He shook his head, his anger slipping free. *"Forty-one."*

Robin's throat constricted. Forty-one seemed old from the perspective of a twelve-year-old. As an adult, she had come to appreciate its relative youth. At forty-one a man had barely entered into his prime. Heads of government that age were considered unseasoned.

"It must have been very hard," she sympathized, once she could speak.

"It wasn't a picnic."

"But . . . you must be very proud. Proud of what he did. To have saved a life!" She unconsciously repeated Bridget's counsel.

His laughter was hollow. "That's what people kept saying."

"Didn't you believe them?"

"I was a little busy at the time."

"Other people might not have done what you did."

"Don't try to fit me into the same mold

117

as my father!" he snapped. "I did what I had to do, nothing more."

The sweet aroma of crushed rose petals wafted in the air. Robin hadn't realized how tightly she'd been holding them until she noticed the scent. Reflexively, she loosened her grip, but the damage had already been done. Just as it had been done long ago to Eric Marshall and his sisters and brothers.

"The girl," she stammered, "the girl he rescued —"

"Shouldn't have been where she was."

"Wasn't she . . . a child?"

"She was twelve! Old enough to know that there are places along the coast where people just shouldn't climb on the rocks."

I wasn't climbing on the rocks! Robin wanted to cry. But she couldn't tell him that. Not without admitting who she was.

"Her parents should have watched out for her a little better in the first place rather than later," he continued mysteriously.

Robin frowned. "I don't understand."

He waved her off. "You don't have to. It has nothing to do with you."

"But if she was just a child —"

"Our father was just as dead! Samantha barely remembers him. David doesn't at all." He motioned to the photo album on the shelf. "All David knows of him is what he's seen in those snapshots. Sometimes I wonder if that's why he is the way he is. If maybe I could have done a better job."

"You did everything you could. I'm sure of that. I haven't met Allison and Benjamin yet, but I know that Barbara and Samantha and even David — yes, David, too — appreciate all that you've done for them."

"Just what do you base that on now? Two weeks' worth of observation?"

Robin lifted her chin. He wasn't going to stop her again with a challenge like that. "Yes," she stated firmly.

Eric glared at her. Then, reining in his anger, he offered an apologetic smile. "Sorry, I shouldn't have let things get so intense. As I said, it has nothing to do with you."

Robin felt as if she'd been held captive on a runaway roller coaster. Up and down, jerked this way and that. It had very much to do with her.

"I — I think I'll go to my room," she said, starting for the door.

"If you change your mind and decide you'd like some company . . ." he began, but didn't finish.

Robin froze.

A second passed, then another, before he murmured faintly, "Such a waste."

Robin couldn't stop herself from turning to look at him. His last words hadn't meshed with the previous challenge. They'd sounded almost . . . wistful.

He stood at the window, holding back the curtains in order to peer outside. But as she very well knew, there was nothing there for him to see.

When she turned away again, he didn't notice.

The sadness that all too frequently descended upon Eric after any discussion of his father held sway as he stared blindly out the window. He missed his father more than he was willing to admit. He'd been an adult when his father died; he should have been past the point of needing him. The children, yes. But he had already achieved manhood. He also missed his mother. Her sweetness, the soft way she had of showing them they were all loved. He harbored no bitterness toward his mother. She would have done anything she could to have stayed with her children. His father, on the other hand . . .

Eric shook his head, rejecting the idea. He didn't like to think that his father might have made a conscious decision to abandon his own children. But whether he had or not, the outcome was the same.

What would have happened if he had held back? If on that fateful day he, like most people, had waited for someone else to act? The girl would most likely have been lost. But then they — his family — would still have their parent. And Eric might be the veterinarian he'd always hoped to become. He might be married. He might have children of his own.

Eric pushed away from the window in disgust. His long-ago dreams had about as much substance as a foggy mist. To keep the record straight, he was a man in the fast lane to solitary, middle-aged innkeeperhood! In a few years, a new photo could be added to the family album: himself, with a nonexistent hairline and a roll of fat settling comfortably around his middle, fussing codgily about the flower beds while he complained to one and all that none of his far-flung family members ever came to visit.

Eric's short bark of laughter chased away any lingering melancholia. When he'd been a young go-getter forming future plans, this certainly hadn't been the lifestyle he'd conceived for himself. Nor was it a particularly appealing prospect today.

CHAPTER SEVEN

The fog burned away rapidly the next morning, saving the coast from a repeat of the day before. With renewed enthusiasm, the visitors to Dunnigan Bay swept out of the inn to explore the countryside. Frank Whittaker and his wife were the last to leave.

"Where did you put the camera, Alma? I distinctly told you to keep track of it. If we don't hurry, we're going to miss the best light. Come on, woman, think!"

Alma thought, came up with an answer that might please her husband, ran upstairs and then back down again, a beaming smile on her long, rather equine face and the camera held victoriously in her hand.

"Atta girl!" Frank Whittaker approved, before he ruined the moment by grouching, "Next time, don't lose it!"

The pair then collected their picnic basket and bustled through the front door.

Samantha heaved a huge sigh of relief as

she slumped into one of the chairs in the kitchen. "What an awful person!"

"Alma needs to stand up to him."

"Alma needs to pack her bags and leave. No note, nothing. Just disappear over the horizon."

Robin smiled. "Is that what you'd do?"

"I wouldn't marry a man like Frank Whittaker in the first place."

"She must love him."

"That's not my idea of love!" Samantha retorted. "It's not yours, either, is it?"

Robin shook her head. "No."

"Bridget says true love is selfless. That you think of the other person — what they want and need, what they feel, what's best for them — before you think of yourself. It has to work both ways, though, not just one person doing all the giving."

"Bridget sounds like a wise woman."

"I do miss her. It's like . . . she's the closest to a mother I've ever had. Since my real mother died, of course," she hurried to add, in case Robin might think she was slighting her birth mother.

"I know what you mean," Robin said.

Samantha relaxed, and gazed out into the garden. So far, the morning sun had illuminated only a small section of plants and flowers. Moisture still clung to the rest.

"Our parents were married shortly after they turned nineteen," Samantha said. "It's so funny . . . here I am, twenty-one, and I can't *imagine* being married. Much less having a year-old child, like they did." She paused. "But I suppose it was a good thing they started early. Considering what happened and all. They didn't have a lot of time, like some people do."

Robin had decided earlier that morning to make the test cake at her first opportunity. After breakfast, she had finally found the time to start gathering the necessary ingredients. But as she listened to Samantha, her actions slowed.

"I'm also the age Eric was when he had to quit college to take care of us," Samantha continued, shaking her head. "I can't imagine doing *that,* either. David was still in diapers! And I wasn't much better. No wonder Eric gets upset when anyone talks about the accident. Bridget says it's not good for him, though. She says it's wrong for a person to keep that kind of anger inside them for too long. But she doesn't say that to Eric anymore. He won't listen."

"Is that why you didn't want him to know what we were talking about last night when he found us looking at the photo album?"

"Yes."

"We talked about it anyway."

"Did he tell you about the girl?"

Robin nodded.

"Then you see what I mean."

"But she was so young!"

"That doesn't seem to matter. It also didn't help that her father came to see Eric a short time after our dad died."

Robin's breath caught. Her father? Had gone to see the Marshalls?

Samantha shook her mane of hair and tied a portion of it up with a ribbon she pulled from her pocket. "I don't remember it, of course, but the story goes that the girl's father showed up one day on the doorstep, check in hand, as if money could make up for the loss of our father. When he tried to give it to Eric, Eric exploded. He threw the man out and told him never to try to contact any member of our family again . . . that we didn't want his blood money . . . that he and his daughter would just have to live the rest of their lives with our father's death on their conscience. Eric didn't know it, but Benjamin was in the next room. He told the rest of us what he heard."

Blood money. Her poor father! He had been a quiet, shy man . . . often having trouble expressing himself. If he had offered the Marshalls money, it had not been as a sop to his conscience, as they thought, but to ease their way. Throughout his life he had helped many people in need. Now she also knew another reason, possibly the primary reason, that her parents hadn't wanted her to initiate any contact with the Marshalls when she was young. They hadn't wanted her to receive the same treatment.

"Did you have a hard time financially?" she asked.

"A fund was started by some people in the community shortly after our father's funeral. Eric made sure, as best he could, that none of the man's money was in it. That was the only way he'd agree to use it. The house was all ours, since Dad had taken out an insurance policy that paid off the loan. We did okay. Then we came up here."

"I . . . I still can't help thinking about the girl."

"Roberta Farrell. That was her name. I often wonder what happened to her. But don't tell Eric I said that! And don't ever mention her name!"

"I won't," Robin promised.

Samantha flashed her a quick smile of camaraderie and then stood up. "Well, I have to get busy. You know Benjamin and Allison are coming up this weekend for David's birthday, right? And the twins? You'll finally get to meet them!"

"Is there going to be a party? For David, I mean."

Samantha shook her head, making her mass of blond hair bounce. "Nothing formal," she said. "Just everyone getting together. Kind of low-key."

"A special meal? A cake?" Robin persisted.

"You'll have to ask Eric. Last year when we tried to have a special dinner, David ended up stomping out halfway through."

When she was alone again, Robin tried to take up where she'd left off but found it difficult.

What did she do now? The situation seemed to be getting more and more complicated. When she'd first come here, she'd vaguely speculated that after a time she might tell them who she was. That is, if things worked out in the way she hoped. Now, the more she became involved in their lives, the more she knew that the matter could never end that simply. If she told them who she was, Eric would instantly dismiss her. And she wasn't ready to leave Heron's Inn yet.

With exaggerated care, Robin placed the large glass bowl into position on the mixer and forced herself to concentrate on her work.

■ ■ ■

For the family, lunch consisted mainly of leftovers from the day before. No particular time was set for eating. Most midday meals were reheated in the microwave and eaten in ones and twos at the small table in the kitchen. Dishes were racked immediately in the dishwasher. Robin had little to do from that point until it was time to start dinner. Often she spent her free time in the garden, tending the little patch of herbs and vegetables that Bridget had planted earlier in the season.

That afternoon, she used the time to continue making the sample decorations for the test cake, her talented fingers shaping delicate-looking petals for sweetheart roses, sweet peas, a large cluster of Dainty Bess roses and the tiny filler flowers of eriostemon. This cake, of course, would be on a much smaller scale than the final version she would prepare for the actual wedding. That is, if her work met with everyone's approval, especially the hard-to-please Eileen.

Tonight, after dinner, she planned to put it all together — the deliciously scented almond white cake and the decorations — then show it to Barbara. Barbara was the person she most wanted to please.

She was transferring the last sugar-flower petals to the counter beside the cooling cake when Eric came up behind her. She hadn't seen him since early that morning. He'd either skipped lunch or been away from the inn.

"If I didn't already know where the kitchen is, I'd have no problem finding it," he said jokingly. "All I had to do was follow my nose." He leaned over to see what she was doing. "That smells wonderful."

"It's Barbara's test cake," Robin replied.

His eyes skimmed the delicate decorations, a few already assembled. "You did all this?"

She went to the sink to wash her hands. "Yes. I told you I once worked at a bakery."

"That must have been some bakery."

"It was." Her replies were terse and a little cooler than she'd intended.

He leaned against the counter. "You're full of little surprises," he murmured.

"Isn't everyone?" She started to clear the counter. She refused to look at him.

"Some more than others," he said.

"Yourself excluded, I suppose?"

"Me most of all. Did you miss me earlier?"

"You were missing?"

He grunted. "That was below the belt!"

"I hit where I have to," she said tightly.

He straightened, frowning, for the first time realizing that something was wrong. "What's going on?" he asked.

"Nothing."

"Something sure is! Last night —" His frown eased as he thought he'd come up with the reason. "You're angry about last night!"

"I'm not angry about anything."

"About what happened."

"Nothing happened."

"That's not the way you felt last night."

"Look!" She turned to him in exasperation. "Can't we just —"

"You say you're not married. Are you involved with someone? Is that it?"

"There's no one else."

"Then what is it? Don't tell me you don't feel the same attraction that I do, because I won't believe it."

"Your ego is outrageous!"

"My ego doesn't enter into it. I'm struggling here, Robin. Trying to understand."

"Maybe you should stop trying so hard."

He dragged a hand through his hair. "This doesn't make any sense!" He started to pace, then stopped directly in front of her. "All right, Maybe I am pushing this too hard, too fast. Maybe I should pull back a little. But I can't ignore the way I feel about you. You're different, Robin. Different from anyone I've ever met. I want to get to know you — really know you."

Robin swallowed tightly. That was the last thing she could let happen. Still, she said nothing.

His gaze searched hers. "By your silence, I'll assume you agree." His hand slid up and down her arm, then he squeezed it and walked away.

For a long period of time afterward, all Robin could do was stare at the empty doorway.

"It's absolutely beautiful!" Barbara breathed hours later, her pale eyes focused raptly on the cake. "I can't believe it. You actually made this?" She turned to Robin for confirmation.

Robin was pleased. "I did."

"Eileen is going to faint!" Barbara pronounced. "She's not going to believe that someone so close to home — I have to call her. She'll want to come over right away. Is that all right? It's not too late for you?"

Robin hadn't been getting a lot of sleep lately, so whether she spent her time upstairs or down didn't matter. "Sure, call her," she agreed. "I don't mind."

"It's eleven o'clock now. She'll be here by eleven-thirty at the latest."

"I don't mind," Robin repeated.

Barbara rushed off to make her call.

Donal Caldwell tottered into the kitchen, carrying an empty teacup. The old man looked fragile, but after observing him over the past couple of weeks, Robin knew he was much stronger than he seemed. He was very quiet and seldom bothered anyone, preferring instead to spend most of his time outdoors with his paints and canvases. The Marshalls treated him with fondness, like an adopted elderly uncle. He was the only guest scheduled to remain at the inn the week of the wedding.

He examined the cake critically, then turned his gaze on Robin, his small dark eyes glittering with interest. "You did this?" he asked, motioning with his teacup to the cake.

Robin nodded.

"You have an artist's eye," he said. "You should do something with it. Not waste it in a kitchen."

Robin smiled. "A person can be an artist in the kitchen, too, you know."

"Waste of time. Everything gets eaten!"

"As long as it's enjoyed first, does it matter?"

The old man shook his head and Robin laughed. He started to smile. "Guess it takes all kinds," he said. "I'm after another cup of tea. I'm trying to finish a book, but I keep falling asleep."

Robin filled the teakettle and put it on a burner to heat. She and the old man had talked briefly several times, but this was the first opportunity they had had for a longer conversation.

He settled in a chair. "You fit in here," he said, unknowingly echoing the verdict of the others. "A lot of young folks wouldn't. They like to have a lot of hustle and bustle around, a lot of noise. And that's fine, nothing wrong with it, if that's what you want. Young David . . . he thinks he wants it. But I'm not so sure he'd be happy once he got it. Benjamin, on the other hand . . . Benjamin's a joker. He enjoys an audience. He'll make an excellent lawyer."

When he paused for breath, Robin commented, "You know the family very well."

"I should. I've been coming here every summer for the past eight years. I was their first guest."

She ventured, "It's really tragic about their father."

He nodded. "Yes. He was quite a man from everything I've heard. Eric's just like him, so they say."

"Who says?" she asked.

"Allison, for one. She says he has the same quiet way about him — strong inside himself, no need to show off." He shot her a look from beneath bushy gray eyebrows. "The kind of man a woman should latch on to, if she can . . . if you know what I mean."

The teakettle whistled. Robin took his cup, rinsed it with warm water and added a tea bag. Then she filled it with the heated water and brought it back to the elderly gentleman.

"Milk or sugar?" she asked.

"Neither one," the old man said, pushing slowly back to his feet. "This wouldn't be a bad place to practice your skills," he suggested. Then, eyes twinkling, he added, "Your cooking skills, too."

Robin blinked, and before she could make a reply he had disappeared into the hall.

Eileen Clarke was everything Robin expected, plus a little more. She arrived at the inn exactly a half hour after Barbara's call, Timothy in tow, and swept through the kitchen like a commanding general. There were no oohs and aahs from her about the cake. Her questions were direct and to the point, even though they did reveal a measure of approval.

"You realize we'll need three layers," she said.

"For the number of guests you're planning, that's correct."

"And one of those little bride-and-groom things for the top."

"I'm sure I'll be able to find one."

"And a groom's cake. We do want a groom's cake."

"I thought chocolate hazelnut, with chocolate icing and clusters of pink buttercream rosebuds." Robin glanced at Timothy and Barbara. The suggestion seemed to please them.

"Mmm. I don't know," Eileen murmured. The woman sent Robin an appraising glance that didn't wholly have to do with the discussion at hand. Robin had thought Samantha to be teasing when she said Eileen had an eye on Eric. Now she wasn't so sure.

Eric entered the room by way of the rear stairs. "I wondered where everyone was. Eileen . . . Timothy? What's going on?"

"We're deciding about the cakes," Barbara answered, suppressed anxiety raising the pitch of her voice.

Eric glanced at Robin, gave her a quick, intimate smile, then turned his attention to the cake. Robin saw his eyes widen. He, too, was surprised by the beauty of the cake set before them. White on white with the palest of pinks, lavenders and yellows in a symphony of clustered flowers. He'd seen most of the decorations before, unassembled, but not artfully applied with swirls and pipings of frosting.

Samantha arrived home from a date and joined everyone in the kitchen. She stopped short when she saw the cake.

"I don't know," Eileen stated, "chocolate for the groom's cake seems so . . . so ordinary."

"If Robin makes it, there is no way on earth a chocolate cake will be ordinary!" Samantha insisted, coming to Robin's defense.

"Chocolate *hazelnut,*" Barbara corrected her mother-in-law to be.

"It's the groom's cake," Eric suggested. "Why don't we let the groom decide?"

Timothy glanced at Barbara, at his mother, then back at Barbara. "I think . . . I think chocolate hazelnut is fine. It sounds delicious, actually."

"But will she be able to do it again?" Eileen demanded. "I mean, yes, this is beautiful. But is it a fluke? What will the actual wedding cake be like?"

136

"Much the same, only more so, with three layers and a bride and groom on top," Robin answered. "This isn't a fluke."

Barbara spoke up. "I'd really rather not have a bride and groom. Instead, maybe a few more of these beautiful flowers?" Her eyes pleaded with her brother to intervene on her behalf.

"Then that's the way it will be," he decreed. He smiled at Eileen before collecting her arm to accompany her out of the kitchen. "Now, see?" they heard him say as he walked with her down the hall. "That's another problem solved."

"But do you really think —" Eileen sputtered. "I mean, who *is* this person? She only showed up here a few weeks ago. Surely we shouldn't trust —" Her words were cut off by their exit through the front door.

"Crabby old cow!"

"Samantha!" Barbara scolded severely. She grabbed Timothy's arm and hurried him into the hall.

"Oops!" Samantha said to Robin, grimacing. "But it's true. She *is* a crabby old cow. She certainly wasn't very nice to you."

"She's under a lot of pressure," Robin observed.

"She asked for it! In fact, she *demanded* it. Just because Timothy is her only child and she's always dreamed of planning his wedding, and just because she says she already thinks of Barbara as her daughter . . . Do you know, if Eric hadn't put his foot down, Barbara would be wearing a dress *Eileen* chose as her wedding gown!"

"Why won't Timothy stand up to his mother?"

"Timothy —" She glanced over her shoulder and lowered her voice. "Timothy hates to make waves. One day he may have to make a choice, though, between Barbara and Eileen. I only hope Barbara wins."

"You're concerned about her."

"She's my sister."

"But you seem never to worry much about anything."

"I think about things. I just don't dwell on them. What good does that do?"

What good indeed, Robin agreed silently.

Samantha yawned. "I'm tired. I think I'll go to bed early tonight. See you in the morning." She started for the rear stairs but stopped with her foot on the first narrow step. "That cake looks as if it belongs on the page of some fancy bride's magazine. It's a pretty amazing job for an amateur." She didn't wait for a reply.

Robin couldn't sleep. She tried for the next

two hours, but she couldn't force her mind to rest. She swung her legs over the side of the soft mattress and searched with her toes for her slippers. Maybe a drink of water would help. Water from downstairs, so she could walk off some of the tension. Wrapping her silk robe tightly around her, she crept down the hall to the servants' stairwell.

A tiny light bulb threw weak light against the high, close walls. The steps were built tightly together and turned three times before finally reaching the kitchen. Robin was thankful she wasn't claustrophobic.

She filled a small glass with water and took several sips, only to find it wasn't what she wanted after all. Restlessly, she crossed to the French doors that opened into the garden. One was slightly ajar.

She hesitated. Was someone else having difficulty falling asleep that night? The worst possibility was Frank Whittaker. If it was Frank, she didn't want to talk to him. She started to turn away but stopped when she saw the silhouette of a man much taller and more athletic than Frank could ever hope to be.

Eric looked up and saw her, then looked away.

It would have to be her decision whether or not to join him.

CHAPTER EIGHT

She took a long time to decide. And even then, once she started outside, she did so hesitantly, as if he were a wild animal she had to approach with caution.

Eric's jaw tightened, but he remained very still, afraid that if he moved she would be frightened away.

She padded softly on the flat stones that made up the garden pathway, then stopped several paces away from him — not quite within reach.

With natural grace, she folded her arms across her chest, her fingers gripping her upper arms. She didn't look at him but at the roses, whose scent was heavy in the chill, moonlit air.

Her hair was tousled, her face devoid of even the small amount of makeup she wore each day. And still she was beautiful.

Eric drew a sharp breath. He couldn't mess this up. When he spoke it was quietly, conversationally. "I like to come out here when I can't sleep. There's something about a garden at this time of night."

She shivered slightly but made no effort to move away. "Yes," she murmured. "It's like that even in crowded cities. In a garden, late at night, all the people seem far away."

He wanted to ask her, which cities, where she had lived before, what she had done. But again, he didn't want to scare her away. She was like a butterfly, her gossamer wings poised for flight. She'd come into his life unexpectedly. She could just as easily fly away.

Several crickets chirped in song. Somewhere, far off, an owl hooted. And beyond it all was the muffled roar of the Pacific.

"I'm not sure I could ever live in a city again," he said, "not after this."

She glanced at him. "How did you find this place? I mean, you didn't just look in the want ads."

He laughed lightly. "Almost. I tried to pick up where our dad left off. He was a real estate agent. I earned my license and tried to sell property. But I wasn't very good at it. Probably because I only did it part-time, when the kids were in school, and probably because my heart just wasn't in it. If a client didn't like a place, I wouldn't try to convince them otherwise. Take it or leave it, that was my motto."

"A rather refreshing attitude for a salesman."

"A few people thought so. Most didn't. I told you, I wasn't very good. Then one day I was looking through a sales brochure and saw Heron's Inn. I drove up here, looked around, brought the kids up the next weekend, and we moved here. End of real estate career, beginning of being an innkeeper."

"Which you like better, I take it."

"Definitely."

He plucked a leaf from a low-hanging tree branch. To keep himself occupied, he began to fold it.

"You did it for David, didn't you?" she asked.

"Mostly. But I thought we all needed a change. Allison was married, of course, with the twins. She stayed in Palo Alto. She and her husband had good jobs at one of the computer chip makers there. She still does, matter of fact. The rest of us packed up and headed north."

"What did you want to do, originally? I mean, before your father — when you were in college."

He tossed the leaf away. "You're asking a lot of questions." She started to turn away but he stopped her. His hand slipped from her arm, though, before he could follow through on what he really wanted to do — hold her with all his strength.

He forced a soft laugh. "It's okay. I was teasing. If you really want to know, I'll tell you. But the answer will come at a price. You have to tell me something about yourself. I've been the one doing all the talking." When she made no reply, he continued, "I wanted to be a vet."

"A veterinarian?" she repeated, surprised.

He shrugged. "Why not?"

"It's just — I never thought — you don't have any pets around."

"We had a dog. A Labrador. She died just after turning fifteen over the Easter holidays."

"Oh!"

"When I was growing up, our house was always full of animals. Our mother took in anything on four legs or with wings. She kept an unofficial mini animal hospital, nursing and caring for the creatures until she could find them a good home."

"Then it's no wonder you —"

"Now it's my turn," he interrupted. "Did you ever have any pets when you were growing up?"

Her body tensed, as it always seemed to

when the subject turned to her. But this question had been innocuous enough. Was she tensing for what she thought might come later?

"A bird, a blue budgie. I named him Mike."

"Why Mike?" he asked, smiling.

"I named him for a boy I had a crush on."

"How old were you?"

"Nine, maybe ten."

"How did it go between you and the real Mike?"

"He moved away. But I still had Mike the budgie."

"Where were you living? In California?"

"No," she replied, but he had the distinct impression that wasn't true.

"When did you move here? To go to school?"

"I enrolled at UC-Berkeley after I graduated from high school. Went for a year. Quit. Went for another year. Quit again. This time I'm more serious about it."

"What did you do when you didn't go to class?"

"This and that."

"Things like working in a bakery?"

"Yes."

"Where are you from if you're not from California?"

A hard shiver racked her slender frame. "Do you think — could we continue this another time? I didn't plan to come outside. I'm not properly dressed."

She rubbed her hands up and down her arms and shifted her weight from foot to foot.

Eric instantly agreed. He knew very well she was using the chill air as an excuse, but he also knew better than to insist that she stay.

He followed her into the kitchen, which they then crossed to the servants' stairs. He knew she didn't want him to follow her into the stairwell, but she didn't know how to prevent him. Eric could have held back, found some reason to remain in the kitchen, but he wanted to continue his observation of her. More precisely, he wanted to remain in her company.

To be closeted together inside the narrow confines of the stairway could have been extremely intimate. She was just ahead of him, the skirt of her bright silk robe swinging from her hips to play about her ankles as she moved from step to step. All he had to do was reach out. Only at the moment, she would probably resist the idea and raise such a ruckus that it would wake everyone in the house. Sound traveled easily at night.

Any sound. He'd also, in a saner frame of mind, promised that he would back off in his pursuit. He'd told her he wanted to get to know her. But how could he do that when she held so much back?

Why? Why was she being so secretive? In a way it was intriguing. But hand in hand with the allure came frustration.

What did she feel it was so necessary to hide?

Robin continued to shiver once she'd reached her room. She shivered even under the extra blanket she had thrown across the bed.

Electricity had coursed through her body as they'd come up the enclosed stairs. She was surprised that he hadn't felt it. But then maybe he had. He'd looked at her for a long, slow moment once they had reached the third floor, before he turned to go to his room.

Why couldn't the past stay buried in the past? Why did it have to come back to haunt people?

She turned her face into Bridget's feather pillow and cried, the sound muffled so that no one else would hear.

David had done his best to ignore Robin

over the last several days, since her rejection of his invitation to go bike riding. Robin pretended not to notice. Finally, the next morning, while she was washing the vegetables she planned to use in a garden marinade for that evening's meal, the boy decided to reestablish contact.

Still dressed in his favorite grungy clothes, his hair a tumbled mass of loose blond curls, a single earring — a silver skull and crossbones at the end of a short chain — dangling from his ear, he sidled up to the counter beside her and showed her his hands, back and front.

She broke off what she was doing to look at them.

When she made no comment, he said, "They're clean. I've just washed them. Show me how to do this stuff." He motioned to the vegetables.

Robin lifted an eyebrow. "Why do you want to know?"

"Do I have to have a reason?"

"Yes, actually, you do."

He turned away. "Then forget it."

Robin didn't look after him as he stomped away. She merely said, "Then you must not have wanted to learn very badly in the first place."

He immediately halted. "I asked, didn't I?"

"It was more of a command. Until Bridget comes back, this is my kitchen, David. I don't respond well to commands."

"If Eric told you to do something, you'd do it."

"Probably. He pays my salary."

"You work for our family. I'm a member of the family."

"When it suits you," she amended.

"I thought you were my friend!"

"Friends don't order friends around."

He frowned in frustration. "All right, all right. I'm sorry. There. Is that okay? Would you like me to go outside and come back in again so we can start over?"

Robin surprised him by smiling. "Why don't you try asking?"

He blinked, frowned fiercely, then said, "Please?"

She handed him a carrot. "Start peeling."

They worked quietly, side by side. His movements were awkward, unskilled. It took him ages to finish even one carrot, but he persisted. He started and finished another. Finally, he asked, "When are you going to show me how to cut these like you can?"

"It takes time, David. You can't expect —"

"This is boring!" he burst out.

"You have to train the muscles in your hands and arms. Not even Digby could play the guitar expertly the first time he picked one up."

"How do you know?" he demanded.

"It's just common sense. I agree that he's very good. He's the moving force behind Black Obsession. But I don't think he's a genius at the guitar."

"Chad Yee is." He named another member of his favorite band.

"He may be. But I'll still bet he had to practice to perfect his ability."

She cut an onion in half lengthwise, peeled it, positioned the flat side down on the cutting board, made a series of parallel incisions partway down its length, working from the bulb end toward the root, then started to cut across those cuts. She kept her movements slow and careful, aware that David was watching her.

"You can go faster than that! I saw you!"

"I thought you might like to see how I did it."

"Can I try?"

"Sure." She placed the other half of the onion on the cutting board. "Make the cuts just like I did. Then curl your fingers and grip the onion gently between your thumb and little finger. While you cut, be careful

149

where you place the knife, use your knuckles as a guide. Draw the knife through from the heel of the blade to the tip. Rock it in short, even strokes and work your way to the root end. Not too quickly! Remember, use your knuckles as a guide."

"Why aren't we crying?" he asked as he neared completion of his effort. "Bridget always cries when she works with onions."

"It's a matter of positioning and of using a very sharp knife. We don't create as many fumes."

"Wow!"

She smiled at him. "Good job."

He eyed his pieces of onion. "They don't look like yours."

"I've been cooking longer than you have."

"What's all this for?" he asked, motioning to the red wine vinegar, the cloves of garlic, the olive oil.

"We're making a vegetable marinade as a side dish for the roast we're going to have for dinner tonight."

"What's a marinade?"

"It's a liquid used to soak — in this case, vegetables — to give them a unique flavor."

"Ugh! Sounds awful."

"Wait until you taste it."

He watched her dice the carrots. "Where did you learn to do stuff like this?"

"A lot of it from my mother. She always loved to cook."

"Is she still alive?"

"Yes."

"Do you see her often?"

"As often as I can. She lives in Canada now."

He tapped the side of his knife point absently on the cutting board. "My mother died when I was a baby."

"I know."

He frowned. "Who told you?"

"Barbara. Samantha showed me a photo of her. Of your father, too."

He shrugged, continuing to tap the knife point.

"It must have been hard for you," she said, "losing both your parents."

The knife blade poised in midair. "How can it be hard when I never knew them?"

"*Because* you never knew them."

He straightened, dropping the knife to the counter and pushing it away. "You sound like one of those school shrinks I used to have to talk to. 'David, tell me how you feel. David, tell me what you think. You must learn to express yourself, David.' Idiots!"

"You don't seem to have much trouble with that now," she murmured.

151

He stared angrily at her for a moment, then the expression in his pale eyes changed. He tossed his mass of hair. "Yeah, you're right. I'm just picky about who I talk to."

She scooped the onions and carrot pieces into a large bowl. "Tell me," she said, opening the bottle of wine vinegar and pouring an appropriate amount over the small mound of vegetables. "Your birthday is Saturday . . . have you thought about what you'd like to do?"

"Go for a bike ride . . . with you."

Robin smiled. "I'd be honored. But what I actually meant was, would you like a special dinner? A cake?"

"Neither."

"But your brother and sister are coming. Your niece and nephew, too. Don't you think they'd all enjoy a celebration?"

"They're coming up a week early for the wedding. My birthday is just incidental."

"I truly doubt that."

"You don't know them the way I do, okay? Just believe me when I say that it doesn't matter. I don't want a dinner, and I don't want a cake."

"May I at least wish you a simple happy birthday on Saturday?"

"*And* come for a bike ride?"

"That, too."

152

"Then it's a deal," he said gruffly, and left the room.

As the week drew to a close, so too did the various guests' reservations. The Whittakers were the first to leave. Frank, true to form to the very end, grumbled that his wake-up call had been five minutes late and, as a result, his plans for the entire day had to be altered. Eric listened patiently, apologized even though he later said the call wasn't late, then gallantly took Alma's hand and kissed it. She tittered and flushed, while Frank looked on grumpily.

The departures of the other guests proceeded smoothly, until finally Donal Caldwell was the only person outside the family and Robin to inhabit the inn.

By Saturday morning the fine tension that came with hosting strangers had dissipated, and breakfast was much more leisurely. Samantha came downstairs in her robe and slippers, Barbara with her hair wrapped in a towel.

"It's a special conditioner," she explained.

"Only one week left," Samantha teased. "Time enough to change your mind."

"I'm not going to change my mind!" Barbara snapped edgily, reaching for a freshly baked cinnamon roll.

153

Samantha grinned. "Nerves starting to kick in, huh?"

Barbara glared at her, then shrugged. "Yes, I guess," she admitted. "I thought it was bad before. If I live through this week, the marriage will be easy."

Eric entered the room, yawning. "What's this about marriage being easy?"

"Especially with Eileen as a mother-in-law," Samantha contributed.

"It's going to be all right. We'll be fine," Barbara defended her commitment.

"Of course you will," Robin agreed, setting a fresh carafe of coffee on the table. Barbara sent her a grateful look.

"Have you eaten?" Eric asked her as she started to turn back to the kitchen.

"Not yet."

"Then come sit down. We're all going to need these few days to relax. You included."

"But —" she protested. He didn't understand that being in the same room with him wasn't a relaxing experience for her. She could scarcely tell him that, though.

"No buts," he insisted. "Toward the end of the week, the place will start to fill up again with the wedding guests. It's going to be more hectic around here than it's ever been. You'll probably be asking me for a bonus."

154

She settled into a chair. This was the first time she had been a participant at the family dining room table. Until now, her meals had always been taken in the kitchen.

"Relax," Eric murmured for her ears alone while his sisters talked. He poured a cup of coffee. "Drink this, eat something and you'll feel better."

"I feel perfectly fine as I am."

"You look as if you've seen our ghost again."

"No."

"You've seen our ghost?" Samantha exclaimed, catching the key word. She frowned in speculation. "For some reason it seems to like the kitchen. What did it do?" she asked curiously.

Robin shrugged. "I never actually saw a form. It was more a movement I caught out of the corner of my eye."

"Bridget says the air vibrates. Are you Irish?"

"Not that I know of."

"See?" She turned to Eric. "It can't only be in Bridget's Celtic imagination, if Robin saw it, too."

"Maybe we should advertise that the place is haunted," Eric teased.

"I think it's Micha Talbot," Barbara said between bites. "He was such a horrible man,

155

he's doomed for all eternity to remain in the place where he caused so much heartache."

Samantha snickered. "Our kitchen?"

"This house. Dunnigan Bay."

"Well," Samantha said, "I think it's the ghost of some poor servant girl who spent hours and hours scrubbing in the kitchen. So many hours that she just can't leave."

Eric laughed outright. "It's a good thing she didn't spend her days scrubbing the entryway. I'd hate to think of how many people would have unknowingly tripped over her."

"Oh, you!" Samantha cried, and threw her napkin at him.

Everyone was laughing when David came to stand in the doorway. His dour look was like a bucket of cold water thrown on their jocularity. Smiles faded or became forced.

"Good morning," Eric said in greeting.

David murmured something unintelligible.

Samantha's gaze darted from brother to brother. "We were talking about our ghost, Davey," she said after a strained moment had passed. "Robin's seen it, too! Tell him, Robin. He's like Eric. He doesn't believe in it, either."

Robin started to deny again that she'd

156

actually seen it but was interrupted by David's hostile reprimand, "Don't call me Davey! You know I don't like it!"

"She didn't mean it as an insult," Eric said evenly.

"Everything anyone says around this place is an insult. I'm eighteen now, okay? I'm an adult. I should be treated like an adult."

"It takes more than reaching a certain age to be an adult," Eric retorted.

"You mean like yourself, right? You were probably born an adult."

"David!" Barbara scolded.

"David, please," Samantha pleaded. "Not today."

"What's different about today? Oh! It's my birthday!" he said sarcastically. "I didn't hear many happy returns of the day when I came in just now. Did you?"

"You didn't give us time!" Samantha cried.

David dismissed her reasoning. "Who cares? It doesn't really matter."

"If you came here looking for a fight —" Eric snapped. He started to rise from his chair.

"I came here to find Robin," David growled. "She and I are going bike riding."

Eric laughed shortly. "Maybe you'd better check with her again. She may have changed her mind."

All eyes switched to Robin. As silent witness to the scene that had just taken place, she knew exactly who had started all the trouble. But she could also see that beneath the boy's bravado lay a tremendous amount of pain. She couldn't turn him down, even if that was her first inclination.

She stood up. "I'll just be a minute."

David's smile lorded his victory over his brother. "Good," he said without looking at her. "I'll be outside." Then he wheeled away from the doorway, leaving everyone in the room to deal with the aftereffects of his antagonism.

Samantha looked at Barbara and then at Eric. She reached out to cover his hand with hers as he settled back into his chair.

Eric shook his head, dismay replacing anger.

"I'll talk to him," Robin offered.

"There probably aren't enough words," Eric murmured.

Their gazes met, and Robin perceived all the years of effort and strain, uncertainty and apprehension, sacrifice and the sometimes dubious rewards that had gone into his struggle to be a father to his siblings. He had done his best, but, as often seemed to be the case with caregivers, it was the hardest to reach who caused the most heartache.

"I'll still try," she said softly.

Something undefinable had passed between them in those moments. A linking of spirits, of souls. He felt it and so did she.

He nodded slowly, and she turned away.

CHAPTER NINE

They rode along the back trails, over isolated hilltops and through hidden glens. When Robin's muscles could stand no more, she called ahead to David for a rest.

He stopped, straddling his mountain bike, and waited for her to catch up. She let her bike coast the last few feet before staggering to a halt. Her cheeks were red, her breathing labored, but her eyes reflected her enjoyment, as did her wide smile.

"That was wonderful!" she cried. "But if I don't stop now, you may . . . have to send up flares to . . . help get me back to the inn."

"Why didn't you say something earlier?" he demanded.

"I was having too much fun."

He swung a leg free and leaned his bike up against a tree. Then, after lending her a helping hand, he did the same with her bike.

"How long has it been since you've ridden?" he asked as she wobbled along the trail.

"The last time I rode I was eighteen, I think," she said. "So about ten years."

"You're going to be sore tomorrow. We shouldn't have come so far."

"I wouldn't trade it for the world. It's been a lovely morning."

They walked to the side of a tiny stream and sat down, Robin already starting to feel stiffness in her muscles. She straightened her legs and began to rub her thighs and calves.

"Eric's gonna be pis— not pleased," he amended in midword.

"What does Eric have to do with it?" Robin asked. "I make my own decisions."

David threw a small stone into the water downstream. "I've seen the way he looks at you. A person would have to be blind not to see."

"He doesn't own me," she said defensively.

"Would you like him to?" David returned quickly.

"I didn't know we came this far to talk about me and Eric."

" 'Me and Eric,' " he repeated in a mocking falsetto.

Robin was unsettled enough in her own mind that she wasn't about to take any ridicule. She struggled to get up.

"I'm sorry," he said. "Don't go."

Robin looked at him, at the misery behind his contriteness, and she knew that he was asking much more than simple forgiveness. David was in sore need of someone he could talk to. And he had decided that she was that person.

She settled down again. A cooling breeze followed the narrow waterway, teasing the hairs that had escaped from the ponytail she'd pulled her hair into before leaving the inn. She drew her knees toward her chin and propped her arms across them. David stretched out on his side on the bracken. For a time, neither said anything. They enjoyed the sounds of the birds playing in the trees and the water gurgling over rocks in the narrow gully.

Finally David broke the silence. "You didn't think I behaved very well this morning, did you?"

"Did you?" she rejoined.

"It's just — they make me so . . . crazy!"

"All of them?"

He looked down at the ground. "Eric, mostly."

"What does he do that gets to you?"

"Breathe?" David joked.

162

"That's not very funny," she admonished gently.

"I know. It's just . . ." He shrugged, unable to put his feelings into better words.

Silence again stretched between them. Robin searched for the right thing to say. Many words battled for precedence on her tongue, but none of them would help.

"What are you going to do?" she asked eventually. "Stay here? Leave?"

"I'd like to leave."

"And do what?"

He didn't answer.

Robin sighed. "It's a tough old world out there right now, David. Even people with plans are having a hard time."

"I'd find something to do."

"What if you didn't?"

"You think I should stay here, then! Get that last credit to graduate, go on to college! Just like Eric tries to cram down my throat!"

"Graduating from high school is so important nowadays. And I'm not saying it because that's what Eric says. I'm saying it because I believe it. As for college —"

"I hate school! I'm not good at it!"

"Then do something else."

He jumped to his feet and stomped through the shallow stream to the other

163

bank, his back to her. "I'm not good at *anything*. Ask Eric. Ask any of them. The only thing I'm good at is —" He bit off the rest of his sentence.

His back was ramrod straight, but Robin sensed that were she to force him to turn around there would be a glimmer of tears in his eyes.

"Is what?" she probed softly.

He raked a hand through his long hair, the gesture reminiscent of his brother when he was feeling uncertain. Wordlessly, David shook his head.

Robin struggled to her feet and limped across the stream. Her muscles were stiffer now than they had been before. She hoped that tomorrow she would be able to get out of bed!

She touched the boy's arm. "There are other things besides college. I have a friend like you who wasn't particularly interested in formal studies. This friend went to a trade school — a culinary school — to learn to be a chef. You could do that, too."

"Yeah, right."

"You could."

He turned to look at her, and she saw that she'd been right when she speculated about the tears. A web of moisture still clung to his eyelashes.

Before she knew what to expect, he bent down to kiss her. It was a sweet, awkward salute that lasted only seconds. When he straightened, he began unevenly, "I said you were different and you are. You're the only person who ever . . ."

She waited for him to finish. When he didn't, she smiled gently. "I believe in you, David. You're smart, you're capable. All you have to do is start believing in yourself."

He shook his head, denying everything she'd said, but she stopped him by catching hold of his chin.

"Don't contradict your elder," she teased him.

A slow smile touched his lips. "You aren't that much elder," he answered.

"Tell that to my poor aching back. Come on. Help me onto my bike before I'm too stiff to bend over."

"Is it that bad?" he asked, genuinely concerned.

She grinned. "I'll live, but I may have to ask you to help me make dinner tonight."

He looked at her. "That's not exactly the height of subtlety, you know."

"I know. Will you do it?"

"On my birthday?"

Robin forged on. "And will you be a little nicer to the others, Eric included? They truly didn't mean to upset you this morning."

"It's *my* birthday. Shouldn't they be a little nicer to *me*?"

"They will if you let them."

"So it's all my fault!" Some of his prickliness was returning.

"I didn't say that."

He frowned, weighing his decision. "All right," he agreed. "But none of them better give me a hard time."

Robin nodded her approval.

The trip back to the inn took longer than the trip out because they went more slowly and took frequent breaks. Once they returned, it was to find that Allison and her children had arrived. Her car, a late-model BMW, was parked in the drive.

"The brats are here," David muttered.

"Are they that bad?"

"Wait till you meet them."

Robin helped David put away the bikes, and as they walked into the house, she tried to brush herself off and straighten her hair. David made no such effort. Voices led them to the living room.

A woman, unmistakably a Marshall, sat in a chair across from Eric. Her hair was cut in a short bob, her makeup applied flawlessly, her dress reflective of style and good taste. She was laughing at something her brother had said, when her attention was drawn to the doorway. She made a soft sound of pleasure, stood up and held out her hands.

David hesitated for only a second before closing the distance to accept his sister's embrace. As he stepped back, her gaze moved beyond him to Robin.

"Robin," Eric said, motioning for her to come farther into the room, "this is our sister Allison. Allison . . . Robin McGrath."

Allison had the most identifiable face, next to Eric's, from Robin's footage. At the time of Martin Marshall's death, she'd been sixteen, second oldest, and her features hadn't changed much over the years.

"I've heard a number of very interesting things about you," Allison said, extending her hand.

Robin accepted it. "Nothing bad, I hope."

"No," Allison murmured. "Very good, as a matter of fact. Barbara tells me you're going to make the cakes for the wedding."

"Yes."

"You're very versatile."

David shifted in place, while Robin moved a sore muscle in her shoulder.

"You were gone a long time," Eric murmured.

"We didn't give you a timetable," David snapped.

Eric continued to look at Robin. "You look exhausted."

"Eric!" Allison reprimanded humorously. "What an awful thing to say to a person."

"She's fine!" David declared, his hostility rising.

Robin placed a hand on David's forearm, a reminder of the promise he'd made. The boy's lips tightened, but he said nothing more.

"What I need most right now is a nice hot bath," Robin said. "David, I had a wonderful time. Thank you for sharing so much of your birthday with me."

"Oh! That reminds me," Allison said brightly, reaching for her purse. She handed her youngest brother a greeting card.

He opened it, and before reading the verse withdrew a check.

"I remember when I was eighteen," Allison explained, "there never seemed to be enough money around to get what I wanted. So I thought a little cash might come in handy for you, too."

"Thanks," David mumbled, awkwardly stuffing the check into a pocket.

He glanced at Robin, at Eric and then at the door. It was easy to see that he wanted to escape.

Robin tried to make things easier for him by underscoring her own departure. "Well, if you'll excuse me . . ."

"Oh, of course!" Allison exclaimed. "It was rude of us to keep you waiting. We'll have a lot more time to talk later. The children and I have decided to stay for two weeks, not one. That doesn't interfere with anything you have planned, does it, Eric?"

"Not in the least."

"Good!" Allison replied.

Robin edged a step closer to the door. Eric saw what she did and excused himself, as well, at least temporarily. "I'll be back," he said. Then to Robin, "There's something I want to discuss with you."

Robin frowned. "What?" she managed to ask as he swept her out of the room alongside him. Her last image was of Allison reaching out to give David another hug before urging him into the chair Eric had abandoned.

They stopped just inside the kitchen.

"Allison insists that we have some kind of dinner for David," Eric said. "She wasn't here last year. She didn't see the way he behaved. She wants to take him out to dinner in Vista Point tonight."

"That sounds like a good idea."

"You won't be upset?"

"Why should I be upset?"

"I've heard you offered to make a special dinner for him yourself."

She smiled, shaking her head. "I won't be upset."

"You're invited."

Again, she shook her head. "This should be a family occasion. Just you and your brothers and sisters. Benjamin will be here in time to go, won't he?"

"He should."

Robin hesitated. "If you meet David halfway, he'll meet you."

"You talked with him?"

"I told you I would."

"What did he say?"

"Not a lot, but he did promise to try. Just don't — Try to be nice to him, too."

"You think I haven't been nice in the past?"

Robin didn't want to hurt him, but he needed to be told the truth. "I think that sometimes you *both* jump to the offensive a little too quickly. Neither of you gives the other person a chance."

"And I'm the oldest. I should know better, right?"

"That's not what I said."

"Do you think I haven't tried?"

"You should try again."

"And then what? What if it doesn't work? I'm not one to admit defeat easily. This is not something I planned."

"You can't control everything, Eric," she said softly. "You can't plan how life is going to turn out. You have to take each day as it comes — each minute."

"You're telling *me* that?" he snapped.

Robin bit her bottom lip to keep from retorting that, yes, she was equally qualified. She had learned that lesson just as cruelly as he. But instead, instinctively wishing to offer comfort, she reached out to touch his cheek.

The feel of him sent slivers of awareness shooting through her body. Sensing danger, she started to move away, but he held her in place.

He pulled her closer. The sensuality that had always hovered in the air between them seemed suddenly to intensify.

"So, it's your philosophy that we should live only for the moment," he murmured huskily. "Take what's offered and forget everything else."

Robin glanced nervously at the open doorway. "Eric, someone could come in."

He bent to tease her lips, almost kissing her, yet not.

Robin's breaths were shallow. Her blood sang through her veins.

The French doors burst open and two children erupted into the room. The doors were quickly pushed shut by four hands that fought to control the knobs. Shrill laughter accompanied their attempt to keep someone out. The same height and weight, one child had brown hair, the other dark blond. One was a girl, one was a boy: Gwen and Colin, respectively.

"Uncle Eric! Uncle Eric, help!" Colin cried. "We have to keep Sam out. She was right behind us!"

Eric seemed reluctant to let go of Robin. Because he was slow to release her, she remained in his arms when Allison hurried into the room.

Allison's gaze slid appraisingly over them before moving on to her children. "Didn't we have a talk about this earlier?" she demanded. "What did we say?"

The twins turned to face her. "That if we aren't considerate houseguests, Uncle Eric will ask us to leave."

"Is this being a considerate houseguest?"

Both sets of blue eyes fell to the floor. "No." There was something of the Marshall

172

look about them, but it had been diluted by other strong genes. Only the color of their eyes remained true.

Samantha rushed into the kitchen by way of the front door. Out of breath from running, she laughed when she discovered her youngest relatives held captive there.

Robin wiggled free of Eric's hold. Still, he persisted in rubbing the inside of her arm with his thumb. He didn't seem to mind that his siblings might notice.

"I won!" Samantha cried. "I touched the stairs before you did," she added in the ageless singsong voice of childhood.

"Samantha, grow up!" Allison admonished. "You're not being much of an example for the twins. I'm trying to civilize them."

Another Marshall arrived on the scene. Benjamin walked into the kitchen, a duffel bag slung over his shoulder. He was almost the same height as Eric and almost as muscled. His blond hair was cut close to his head, and his features were somewhat finer. "What?" He pretended amazement. "You're trying to civilize the brats?"

He tossed the duffel bag into a corner and squatted down so that the children could run into his arms. Much laughter and squealing followed, which made Allison raise her eyes to heaven, as if petitioning for divine guidance.

Benjamin stood up, hugged Allison and Samantha, then came over to Eric with a big smile. He thumped him hard on the shoulder, then gave him a hug, too.

"Who's this?" he asked of the room at large when he drew back and saw Robin.

"Robin McGrath," Eric answered. "Bridget's summer replacement. And before you get any ideas, she's already spoken for."

"That's some fairly fast work, bro," Benjamin complimented, exchanging a look of masculine approval with his brother.

Robin shook herself free of Eric's claim, both physically and verbally. "*No one* should get any ideas," she corrected him. "Hello, Benjamin."

"You know my name."

"It would be hard not to. I've heard it often enough."

"Did they tell you that one day I'm going to be an up-and-coming young attorney who drives a fast car and has lots of money to spend on fun things?"

"I believe I heard something to that effect."

"Good." Benjamin drew out the word. "Maybe you'd be willing to wait around? It'll only take me about five or six years to

174

get there."

Robin grinned. "I'll think about it."

Benjamin had come a long way from the child who had cried so despondently in Robin's footage. Seeing him happy and seemingly well adjusted lifted a portion of the weight she had carried through the years. His piteous tears had spoken so eloquently for all of them. If he could be truly happy, why couldn't it happen for all of them, herself included?

"Mom! Mom! Can Colin and me go play on the pier?" Gwen inserted in the tiny silence that followed.

"*I . . .* Colin and *I,*" Allison corrected.

"Can we?" Gwen persisted, undeterred.

"Not alone."

"I'll go with them," Eric offered.

The ten-year-olds whooped and ran over to jump on their uncle. He grinned at Robin, then laughingly adjusted one child under each arm. Instead of going down the hall to the front door, he took them outside through the garden, the opened French doors wide enough for three.

"Don't let them get into any trouble!" Allison called after them.

"Trouble and the brats go hand in hand, don't they?" Benjamin teased.

"I shudder to think how it'll be when they

175

turn fifteen," their mother said.

Robin eased out of the room, unnoticed, as the others continued to talk.

Later, as she lay in the tub and soaked her aching muscles with successive additions of hot water, Robin thought about what she'd seen and done in the last hour. The family was now complete. All surviving members had been accounted for and introduced to her. And funny thing . . . she liked them. Not because she felt she had to, either. Under other circumstances, she would have liked them just as well. She felt the strength of their family unit. The way they stuck together.

What would they think if ever they learned the truth about her? Would they feel betrayed?

Now she knew how a traitor or a spy must feel. Day after day, living a lie . . . yet still going on. Because once the route was embarked upon, there was no possible way to go back.

That night, only Robin and Donal Caldwell remained at the inn, the others having gone to Vista Point for David's birthday dinner. As she cleared away the remains of the light meal she and Donal had shared, Robin spared frequent thoughts for what might be happening in the town up the coast. Would David make it through this meal without walking out? Was he trying to get along? Was Eric?

David hadn't been pleased to learn about the dinner. He hadn't been pleased when Allison chided him into wearing something more appropriate than his usual jeans and T-shirt. He hadn't been pleased, either, when Robin told him she wasn't going. But he'd accepted her plea of sore muscles, even to the point of unearthing a heating pad from a storage closet.

Robin actually felt much better after her long soak. Tomorrow she would probably still be sore, but it wouldn't be as bad as she had once feared.

"Wait till you get to be my age," Donal said with bright, teasing eyes as he patiently tried to teach her to play cribbage. "I've found bones and muscles I didn't even know I had when I was young, and they create such a protest at times when I haven't done anything to rile them. You're young. Enjoy life. There's enough time tomorrow for aches and pains."

"Being sore was more of an excuse than anything," she murmured.

"I thought so. To get young David to go

without you. That boy's certainly taken a shine to you."

"I like him, too."

"What about his brother?"

"Benjamin?" Robin feigned ignorance. "I don't actually know him very well yet. We just met."

Donal tsked and shook his head.

Robin grinned. "What is this? Are you a professional matchmaker on the side? Painting isn't enough for you?"

Robin's fondness for the older man continued to grow the more she saw him. He kept to himself at most times, starting out in the mornings with paints and easel and returning in the evenings with a contented smile. She'd seen the painting he was giving to Barbara and Timothy for their wedding: a view of the coastline where they had met. In it, he'd shown a surprising ability with color and his own unique style.

His smile was grandfatherly. "I'd just like to see Eric settled. He's given up a lot for those kids. Mind you, I've never heard one word of complaint from him. But I know it's been at a high cost. Why do you think he's not married? Not because he didn't have the opportunity. I remember once or twice . . . I thought the next summer when I came up here, he'd have a wife. But it just never seemed to work out. The women must have been scared off by the prospect of so many youngsters underfoot."

Robin was uncomfortable with the idea of Eric and other women. Once, she had wanted him to have married, to have had someone with whom to share life's burdens. But now she didn't like to think of him being close to, touching or kissing anyone else.

Then realization hit. She didn't want to think of Eric with someone else because she wanted him herself! She wanted to be the center of his thoughts, the sole object of his desire. Because she loved him?

Her attempts to deal with the chaotic thoughts that followed were not conducive to learning a game of cards, and Donal won each successive hand with gleeful ease.

Robin was upstairs, in bed and staring at the darkened ceiling, when she heard the family's cars arrive back at the inn. From the happy sounds of conversation that floated up to the third floor, she deduced there had been no trouble at dinner. For all their sakes, Robin was glad.

She heard a laugh. Eric's laugh. She would know it anywhere. She imagined how he looked in his dark suit, white shirt and claret-colored tie. Achingly handsome. Just

179

as he had been earlier.

If she wanted to, she could seek him out. But how could she do that? Especially now, suspecting what she did and being who she was.

Robin turned over and hugged the cool pillow to her midsection. It offered little comfort.

CHAPTER TEN

"So! Tell me about her," Benjamin said as he slumped into the chair that Eric used at his desk and swiveled it to face him.

Eric stood at the wardrobe and slipped his suit pants across a wooden hanger. "What do you want to know?" he asked.

"Who she is, where she came from . . ."

"I'm afraid I can't help you much there. I've told you her name. That's about all I know."

Benjamin frowned as Eric positioned his dark jacket over the pants and hung them up. He reached for another hanger and, seconds later, stepped into a pair of sweat pants.

"How did she find out about the place? About the job?"

"She answered our ad in the newspaper."

"What about her references?"

"I didn't ask for any."

Benjamin stared at him.

Eric tossed the white shirt he'd been wearing onto the bed and turned to select a sweatshirt from a wardrobe drawer.

"Was that very wise?" his brother asked at last.

"I haven't acted wisely about her from the beginning." He pulled the sweater over his head and adjusted its fit. "But she does her job well. I don't have any complaints. In fact . . ."

"In fact what?"

"She does it a little too well. She's a much better cook than this place needs. She could get a job anywhere, probably for a lot more money. So, why here?"

"That's another form of the question I asked you."

"I wish I knew the answer."

Benjamin hesitated. He couched his next query with humor. "You aren't trying to tell me you really care for her, are you?"

"I think maybe I am."

Benjamin sat forward. "Whoa! Wait! You say you don't know anything about her, yet you admit —"

"Stranger things have happened."

"To you?"

"Strange things happen to me all the time. We don't exactly live a normal existence. We haven't for years."

"What do the others think of her?"

"Barbara and Samantha have taken to her like a long-lost friend. And she has David almost eating out of her hand."

"I did notice he wasn't as argumentative. He was quiet, but we made it through the meal."

"He talks to her."

Benjamin lifted an eyebrow. "A regular paragon of virtue."

"Law school is making you too skeptical."

"And who taught me to be skeptical in the first place? That's why it blows my mind that you hired her without knowing the first thing about her."

"Sometimes a person just has to take another person on trust. Why should her reason for being here be anything but innocent? This isn't exactly a hellhole. People do pay good money to vacation here. Maybe she just needed to get away from her regular routine for a while. Maybe she needed a change of scenery."

"Maybe she's running away from something . . . or someone."

"I've thought of that, too."

"I'm surprised she didn't at least offer any references."

"Oh, she did. I told her I didn't want to see them."

"Hmm," Benjamin breathed.

Eric smiled. "Come on. Let's go get that exercise you talked about earlier. We both need to walk off dessert."

Benjamin rose slowly from the chair. "I hope you know what you're doing, Eric."

"Does anyone in love *ever* know what they're doing?"

All Benjamin could do was shake his head.

Robin was in the kitchen, starting to clear away the remnants of breakfast, when Allison stepped purposefully to her side and began to help. She emptied the leftover coffee from the two carafes, put away the butter and milk and added several plates to the dishwasher.

When Robin was ready to start hand-washing the knives and the baking pans that didn't fit easily into the dishwasher, Allison procured a tea towel.

"You don't have to do this, you know," Robin said. "There's not really that much left."

Allison, who was just as nicely turned out today in a pair of sleek black slacks and a white eyelet blouse as she had been the day before, responded, "Nonsense. I always try to lend a hand. Bridget would chide me for getting lazy if I didn't."

"I won't tell, if you'd like to take this morning off."

"Would you rather I didn't help you?" Allison asked, pausing.

"No, not at all. I enjoy having company in the kitchen." Robin plunged her hands into the hot soapy water. A certain uneasiness had descended upon the room with Allison's arrival. It was apparent to Robin that she was suspicious of her.

"Those rolls you made for breakfast were delicious," Allison said.

"Thank you." Robin placed a rinsed knife in the dish rack.

"Samantha tells me everything you make is wonderful."

"Samantha sometimes exaggerates."

A smile played about Allison's lips as she dried the knife and put it away. "That's true, but she meant it this time. Eric backs her up."

"I enjoy cooking," Robin said simply.

"It seems that we're very lucky to have found you."

Robin made no comment. Her nerves had started to tighten. This conversation was taking on the feel of a third degree. She washed another knife before submerging a baking pan.

"I understand that you're a student," Allison said. "Which college do you attend?"

"Saint Mary's, outside San Francisco in the East Bay."

"What are you majoring in?"

Robin searched quickly for a subject. "Business management."

"Do you have plans to open your own restaurant?"

"I don't — I'm not sure. I . . ."

Allison paused, holding the pan in front of her. "I'm being very rude, aren't I?"

Robin couldn't think of a suitable answer.

Allison laughed. "Go ahead. Tell me. Even my best friends say I have an inquisitive mind. They phrase it that way to try to keep from hurting my feelings."

"Well . . ."

"My ex complained I was too suspicious of people, but then I caught him cheating on me, so I had grounds."

"I'm sorry."

Allison shrugged. "It happened too many years ago to worry about now. He's married to someone else, I have a great boyfriend and the kids have managed to get on with their lives without having to carry too many scars. Kids are remarkably resilient, though. And if anyone should know that, it's us. You're aware of our family history, aren't you?"

186

Robin nodded.

"We even had the press to contend with," Allison continued. "It was horrible. They were like vultures. Dad's body wasn't even cold yet, and they were at the door wanting a story. One of our neighbors, supposedly over to help, let a reporter talk her way inside. She lined us up on the couch and started filming, when we'd barely registered the fact that he was dead. I'm sure we all looked completely stunned. In the end, Eric threw them out, including the neighbor."

Robin automatically scrubbed the same section of pan as that particular snippet of film played in her mind: the offspring of Martin Marshall sitting on and around the couch as the reporter, Jade Patrick — she remembered her name! — callously pressed for an interview.

"After everyone left," Allison went on quietly, "we just sat there and cried. Then we had to face facts. I don't know what I'd have done without Eric. I was sixteen. I kept trying to act like an adult, but I felt like a very young child. I wanted my dad back. I wanted my mother."

All pretense of washing dishes stopped. Robin stood in place, frozen.

"Eric kept us together. He didn't let us shatter. He didn't let the state come in and put us in separate homes. I tried to help him, but I was having such a hard time myself . . ." She was silent a moment, then she pulled herself from the past to look levelly at Robin. "I'm telling you this so you'll see how much Eric means to us, to me. I don't want to see him hurt anymore. He lost out on enough when he chose us over himself — over what he'd planned to do, what he wanted. I love him. I love him fiercely. And, if necessary, I'll protect him like a she-wolf!"

From the steadfastness of Allison's pale eyes, from the tenseness of her stance, Robin knew she meant every word.

"So, if you're just playing with him, don't," Allison stated.

Robin moved jerkily to rinse her hands. She drew an unsteady breath.

Allison seemed to know when to back off. She mused curiously, "I wonder what the twins are up to. Maybe I'd better find out. That is, if you don't mind . . ." She motioned to the pan in the soapy water.

"N-no," Robin stammered.

Allison's smile was easy, back on track with her earlier friendliness. "Bridget would order me to finish what I started. She'd say that if I'd raised the twins with any sense of decorum, they wouldn't be so apt to get into

188

trouble. Bridget's a dear, but she's never had children. She doesn't understand how the little darlings develop minds of their own. We seem to be in a continual battle of wills." With an airy wave, she left the kitchen.

The room felt unnaturally quiet after Allison's departure. Robin could hear the refrigerator's motor humming. She could hear the slow drip of water from the faucet she must have neglected to shut off properly. She could hear someone walking across the floor in the guest room above.

The trap she'd made for herself was drawing tighter. No matter which way she turned, she faced trouble. She wasn't playing with Eric! Yet if she loved him, as she strongly suspected she did, was there a future in that love? Even if he came to love her, too, could she tell him who she was? And if she did, would he still love her?

Her questions seemed to have no easy answers.

The twins ran into the kitchen. "Uncle Eric! We need Uncle Eric! There's a bird — have you seen him?" Their voices were on the same pitch. It was hard to tell one from the other.

"He isn't upstairs?" Robin asked.

189

"We've been there!" Gwen cried, distraught.

"What is it? What's happened?" Robin squatted down to comfort the little girl.

"A bird! There's a bird all caught up in something! It's jumping around, trying to fly, but it can't!" Colin shuddered as he imparted the information.

Robin offered comfort to him, as well.

"We have to find Uncle Eric," Gwen repeated.

The front door closed and the twins jerked out of Robin's arms. "Uncle Eric! Uncle Eric!" they screeched as their feet pounded down the hall.

Robin heard Eric's quick, concerned reply, then the twins' agitated explanation. The door instantly closed behind them.

It was impossible for her to stay behind. After a quick check to see that what she was working on could be left, she hurried after them.

They were half a block ahead of her, running toward the beach. Gwen had hold of Eric's hand, leading him to the spot. Finally, they stopped near the line where the dune grass grew.

"There!" Colin's high-pitched voice carried on the breeze. "It's right there! See, Uncle Eric! See?"

Eric dropped to his knees just as Robin caught up with them.

Both children were chewing their bottom lips, staring at the young sea gull who had become enmeshed in a set of plastic drink rings. Alarmed by their arrival, the bird struggled to get away, looking pathetically frail. Several of the thin plastic circles had gotten twisted around its body, and one wing and a leg were hoisted in the air.

If the twins hadn't found it, Robin doubted if the bird would have survived much longer. She made a small sound of distress.

Eric withdrew a folding knife from his jeans pocket and handed it to her. Then he leaned forward, wrapping his capable hands gently around the bird to halt its struggles and keep it from injuring itself further.

"Is it hurt bad, Uncle Eric? Is it going to be all right?" the twins demanded.

Eric brought the bird close to his body, using his flat stomach as a brace. "Open the second blade and give the knife to me," he directed Robin. Then, very carefully, he slit the pieces of plastic until the bird was free.

"Are we going to let him go?" Colin asked, still agitated.

"Not right now," Eric said. "He's too weak. And he could be hurt."

"What are we going to do with him, then?" Gwen questioned.

Eric glanced at Robin, at the oversize white shirt she wore over a pair of black leggings. "First, we need to get him warm. Robin, can you hold him for a second while I . . ."

"Of course," Robin answered swiftly. She reached for the bird, who fluttered weakly in her hands.

Eric stood up, shed his blue denim shirt, then pulled the black T-shirt he wore underneath over his head.

It was an odd feeling for Robin to watch him partially disrobe. She'd suspected that his body was well muscled; she'd already experienced his strength. But this was the first time she'd seen him with so little on. A smooth line of sinew and bone curved with masculine grace from his trim midsection to his powerful shoulders. A fine sprinkling of chest hair, only a little darker than the hair on his head, glistened in the sunlight.

Then her gaze was drawn to something else. Around his neck he wore a chain, and from the chain hung a tiny gold medal.

Robin blinked, her appreciation of his body interrupted. The medal. She had seen one like it somewhere before. . . .

Eric slipped back into his shirt and

reached for the bird with the T-shirt spread open between his hands. Before the bird quite knew what was happening, it had been wrapped in the material still warm from Eric's body. "Now we need to find an empty box," he said. "Run to the house, look in the utility room off the kitchen. There should be one on the bottom shelf."

The twins sped into action, their legs flashing as they hurried back to the inn.

Robin stared at the bird. She still felt all wobbly inside. From the sight of the injured bird? From seeing Eric so intimately? From noticing the medal? She couldn't settle on one reason. "Will it be all right?" she asked after a moment.

"I hope so."

"What will you do with it? Can you — I mean, you wanted to be a vet. Can you do something to save it?"

"Luckily for the bird, there's a lady down the coast who treats wildlife. She's the expert. I've brought animals with worse injuries than this to her. The vet in Vista Point even refers to her."

"You've brought other animals to her?"

"A bird or two like this, one that was all tangled up in fishing line. A sick sea otter, a sea lion someone had shot."

"Shot?" she echoed.

193

"It happens once in a while. People either do it for fun or because the sea lions are infringing on their fishing territory."

"But don't the sea lions have first right?"

"You'd think so, wouldn't you? But then you'd also think that people would be a little more conscientious about their waste. All it takes is a few seconds to cut these plastic drink rings apart, or for fishermen to collect their used fishing line. It would save a number of birds and animals a tremendous amount of suffering, even death."

Robin could only stare at him. "This means a great deal to you, doesn't it?"

"I care about animals."

"And birds."

He smiled, then he checked the bird. "Where are those kids?" he said, starting to frown.

"They're coming," Robin answered. She'd seen them burst through the inn's front gate.

Eric punched holes in the top of the box the children brought, then settled the bird in the nest made by his T-shirt.

"All right. Let's get going," he said. "The quicker we do this the better."

Robin walked with them to the Jeep Cherokee. Eric saw the children into the back seat and placed the bird on the floor between them.

"Keep the lid closed," he cautioned them. Two pairs of earnest blue eyes signaled agreement. Then he opened the passenger door for Robin. "Hop in," he invited her.

Robin shook her head. "Unless you need me, I'd better not. I was in the middle of something in the kitchen."

A moment passed. "There's absolutely no question about my needing you," he said quietly.

Robin knew that he wasn't talking about needing her help with the bird. For some silly reason — it wasn't in her nature to blush easily — she felt her cheeks grow hot. And because it was so out of character, she felt all the more embarrassed.

He tipped up her chin and held it between his forefinger and thumb while he studied her flushed face. Then he gave her a short, hard kiss that rocked her to her toes.

"Remember that," he ordered, before he closed the passenger door and circled around to the driver's seat.

If she hadn't thought she loved him before, it would be impossible not to think it now. He was a good man, a caring man, the kind of man she had always dreamed of meeting.

Only why, oh why, did he have to be Martin Marshall's eldest son?

When Robin returned to the kitchen, she found David hard at work cutting the vegetables she'd left out on the counter.

"I thought, since you weren't here . . ." he murmured. "The twins said something about a hurt bird?"

David acted slightly embarrassed that he had thought to assist her, but proud at the same time that he was getting along so well. He'd already finished the two onions and started on the carrots.

"Eric's taking them to some woman down the coast."

"Mrs. Carter," he said, then changed subjects. "I wasn't sure if you'd want me to do the carrots, but I thought, 'Why not?' "

Robin washed her hands before handling any food. It was a habit she never actually remembered learning but something she had done all her life — probably at the insistence of her mother, who had started her cooking shortly after she could walk. Robin remembered clearly helping to make sugar cookies for her third birthday party.

She inspected David's efforts. "You're doing very well," she said. "But you'll find it easier to hold the knife this way." She adjusted his grip. "See how that works."

David made a few cuts, then grinned broadly. "Works great!" he approved.

"I'll turn you into a cook yet," she teased.

His smile slowly disappeared. "Do you think you could?" he asked seriously.

Robin held his gaze. "Is that what you want?" she asked.

He sighed and made a few more cuts. Finally, he shrugged. "Sounds as good as anything else I've heard lately. Eric says I don't think about tomorrow, but I do. Maybe it's because I do think about it that I get so depressed. Is it going to be any better tomorrow than it is today? One thing I know for sure — if I go to college, it won't. I'll hate that, just like I hate it here."

"Why do you hate it here so much?" Robin asked, pulling up a chair. "It's so beautiful."

"I was never consulted."

"How old were you when all of you moved here?" Robin asked.

"Ten."

"The same age as the twins."

David was very still. "Yeah."

"Do you think they're old enough to make decisions like that? I mean, if Allison thought it would be beneficial for them to move up here —"

197

"It's not the same thing. Anyway, I still think they should be asked their opinion. Kids aren't dumb."

"Do you believe Eric thinks you're dumb?" She used the same word as he did, even though she thought it harsh.

"The reason we came here is because they were getting ready to put me into a special school for dumb kids. So I must be dumb, right?"

"Is that what Eric told you?"

"It's what I heard a teacher say."

"You *aren't* dumb."

"I failed two classes last semester."

"Did you study?"

"No."

"Well then?" Robin sent him a cajoling smile.

He started to smile himself. "The counselor at my high school said I'm troubled."

"People do like to apply labels to you, don't they?"

"But I'm not the only one troubled in this family. Eric blames the girl who he thinks killed our dad *and* he blames our dad because he left us. Allison is suspicious of everyone, to the point of driving her husband away. Barbara puts up with Timothy's mother because she's afraid of losing Timothy. Samantha can't settle at anything. She

198

was going to be a forest ranger, then she decided to be a travel agent. Now she's talking about becoming a flight attendant. But she's still *here.* Benjamin . . . I don't know what Benjamin's problem is, but I'm sure he has one. I told you a long time ago that we're all crazy."

Robin didn't know that Eric blamed his father for leaving them. She wondered how David knew that? She doubted that Eric would have told him anything. But David was very perceptive. Possibly too perceptive for his own good.

"Is that the reason you want to become a chef?" she asked. "Because you think you can't do anything else? Becoming a chef isn't easy, David. My friend —" She hated to continue to lie to him. "My friend said it was a lot of hard work. You have to study if you want to be accredited. It does mean more time in school."

"I'd rather learn about cooking than algebra and French."

Robin smiled. "If you learn classical cooking, you'll use plenty of French terms. *Mirepoix,* that's what these vegetables you've been preparing are for — the vegetables used in making a stock. When you cut vegetables in one-eighth-inch cubes, it's called *brunoise.* When you cut them in one-sixteenth-inch cubes, it's called *fine brunoise.* See what I mean?"

"How do you know all of this?"

She shrugged. "I helped him study."

"Was he your boyfriend?"

"Just a friend, okay?"

"Maybe I should tell Eric he has competition."

"Maybe you'd better not." She switched quickly to a different topic. "Tell me, did you have a good time last night?"

David went back to cutting carrots. "It was tolerable."

"What did you have to eat?" She bit her tongue after asking that question. It was too revealing of her keen interest in what people were served in various restaurants. And she'd already given away enough.

"Some kind of poached salmon. It was pretty good."

"Did everyone treat you better?"

"I suppose. No one said anything to irritate me."

"Not even Eric?"

"No."

"Did you get any presents?"

"Benjamin gave me a wallet. It's pretty nice. Eric, Barbara and Samantha bought me a pair of in-line skates, with all the gear that goes with them."

"That sounds like fun."

"Not a lot of places to use them up here."

Allison came into the room frowning. "Have either of you seen Colin and Gwen? They seem to have disappeared."

"They went with Eric to Mrs. Carter's," David answered. "They found a hurt bird."

"Oh?" An eyebrow disappeared into Allison's perfectly feathered bangs as she watched her youngest brother work.

"David is helping me," Robin explained. She couldn't help being uneasy around Allison. She hadn't needed David's assessment to know of his sister's suspicious nature. The woman had admitted as much earlier, when she'd issued her warning.

"So I see," Allison said, and had the good grace not to say anything more.

David was at a delicate stage. Any offhand comment could be taken the wrong way and destroy the fragile confidence that Robin was trying to build.

"Well, when they get back, will you tell them I'd like to see them upstairs?" Allison requested.

"Certainly," Robin replied.

Allison gave a short nod and turned back into the hall.

"The brats are in trouble," David murmured after a moment.

201

"What makes you say that?" Robin asked.

"She keeps them on a pretty tight leash."

"But I thought —"

"They manage to get into trouble anyway."

"Maybe Eric can intervene for them."

David laughed mockingly. "Sure, Saint Eric."

Robin stood up. "You're being too hard on him, David." She pushed several stalks of celery toward the cutting board. "Cut these about the same size as what you've already done."

David's technique was improving. As a result, he didn't take long to complete the assignment. When he was done, Robin swept all the diced vegetables into a tall pot in which she'd already placed the bones of several chickens. She then added water and the sachet of spices she'd prepared earlier, and adjusted the flame on the stove for a quick boil.

She turned back to David. "Don't you think he should stick up for the kids, especially considering the circumstances?"

"Yeah, I guess so," he admitted.

"You would, wouldn't you?"

David studied the floor. "Yeah."

She came to stand beside him, copying his stance by leaning back against the counter and folding her arms. "Aren't you curious about what we're having for dinner tonight?"

"I thought we were having boiled chicken bones," he teased.

Robin thumped him lightly with her elbow. "We're making chicken stock. It's to use with the recipe for corn chowder I found in Bridget's cookbook. The corner of the page was folded down, so I thought it must be a favorite."

"It is."

"In a couple of hours, would you like to help make it?"

"Sure," he said.

"I also thought we'd have apple pie for dessert."

"Better and better," he said, licking his lips.

"I'll see you at three, then."

"I'll be here," he said.

Robin found herself humming as she cleared the counter in order to make several round loaves of hearty wheat bread to accompany the meal. She paused, registered the fact that she'd been humming, then gave herself permission to continue.

CHAPTER ELEVEN

That evening the chowder won high praise, as did David when Robin informed everyone he had assisted her. David tossed his head and acted as if he didn't care what the others thought, but Robin could see that, deep down, he basked in the approval of his siblings.

"What about the sea gull?" Barbara asked. She had come in late to the meal after an afternoon spent chasing after more last-minute wedding details. "Before I left, I heard you took one to Mrs. Carter."

"She thinks it will be fine," Eric answered. "In a few days it will be back out with all the other birds, right, kids?"

Colin and Gwen nodded enthusiastically.

"She has a baby deer that hurt its leg and a falcon with one eye and a whole lot of other animals and birds."

"It's like going to a zoo, only different!" Colin added.

"Someone still should have told me what you were doing," Allison complained. "Rather than make me search all over, thinking the worst."

The twins looked down at their dessert plates. Obviously they'd been chastised.

"They didn't have time, Allison," David surprised everyone by saying.

"That's right," Eric agreed, trying not to look too startled. "Every second counts in an emergency."

"Robin knew," Allison charged.

"Robin was there."

"Someone still should have told me."

"If it happens again, we will. That's a promise," Eric said.

Allison looked somewhat mollified as she ate the last of her pie.

"What's next?" Samantha asked, breaking into the remaining cloud of discontent. "The rehearsal dinner is Friday. What's left?"

"The earliest out-of-town guests planning to stay at the inn will start to arrive Thursday," Eric said. "Robin, this is your last chance if you'd like to spread out a little. You can have one of the large guest rooms in front for a few days, if you like."

"I'm happy where I am, thanks."

"Has Aunt Rachel decided to come?" Samantha asked.

"The last I heard, yes," Barbara answered.

"She's our only close relative," Samantha explained to Robin. "She lives in Idaho."

"She's our *batty* aunt from Idaho," Benjamin corrected, laughing lightly.

"She writes poetry," Samantha retorted.

"Weird poetry," Benjamin said. "But it was worse when our uncle was alive. He used to publish her work and give it away. Then they started to make these pottery balls that had her verses inside. Remember when they sent us a box full of them one Christmas? It took us ages to figure out what they were."

"I remember we found out when you snuck up behind me while I was cleaning the big mirror in the front room. You scared me half to death!" Samantha grumbled, pretending to still feel aggrieved. "You were wearing a costume from a play you'd been in at school. Only you'd altered it until you looked like some kind of hideous monster. I screamed and jumped and knocked off two or three of those pottery balls Allison had set out on the mantel."

"I thought if we kept them out for a respectable period, we could put them away without guilt," Allison said.

"I got the idea to scare you from some TV

show I used to watch," Benjamin said.

"I always knew you watched too much TV," Allison grumbled.

"Maybe it was a 'Partridge Family' rerun," Benjamin mused.

"It certainly wasn't 'Law and Order'!" Samantha said laughing.

"No, 'Law and Order' came later, after I'd decided I wanted to be a lawyer."

"What's 'Law and Order'?" Colin piped up.

"My children aren't allowed to watch TV," Allison explained to Robin.

"Which is probably a good thing," Eric said. "Just imagine what things they'd get into if they did."

Colin turned to Eric. "What is it?"

"It's a show about cops and lawyers on that funny-looking box you sometimes see in other people's living rooms."

"We know what a TV is!" the twins exclaimed, defending their degree of sophistication.

"We watch it over at Billy Winslow's house," Gwen added, then clapped a hand over her mouth as her brother turned to glare at her.

"I'll have to have a little talk with Billy Winslow's mother," Allison remarked.

"Give the kids a break!" David admon-

207

ished, once again surprising them. Surprising even himself, it seemed. He shrugged and mumbled, "You can't hide them from the world."

Allison stared at him, uncertain whether to snap back or smile at the fact that he, David, had acted like a participating member of the family.

"I agree with David," Barbara said. "When Timothy and I have children, we plan to monitor what they watch, but we aren't going to keep them away from it totally."

Eric reached out to cover one ear of each twin. They sat on either side of him, so it was easy. "I agree with both of you," he said, then grinned at the children and removed his hands. "But Allison sets the rules in her house. If she says no TV, then it's no TV. And you kids should do as your mother asks."

"But we don't watch it at home," Colin responded with the crystal-clear logic of a child. "We watch it at our friend Billy's house."

Everyone at the table started to laugh. Even David.

Colin and Gwen were a little mystified at first, but they soon joined in, Colin with added gusto because everyone seemed to think he had made such a fine joke.

As the meal drew to a close, Robin pushed away from the table and began to gather dishes, starting with her own.

Eric stopped her. "I told you when you first came here that whenever the house is full of family, we all pitch in. You and David cooked the meal, the rest of us will clean up."

Robin looked up at him. It was difficult for her to hide her feelings. All through dinner she had studiously avoided giving him more than a quick glance. Yet she'd been keenly aware of him. Aware of the way he quietly headed the family. Aware of the way he interacted with the twins — humoring them, teasing them. If he had children of his own, he would undoubtedly treat them the same way.

"That's right," Barbara agreed. "You should take the evening off."

"But I have all of tomorrow free."

"And this evening, too!" Samantha said with a grin as she eased the plate from Robin's hand. "Isn't that lovely?"

Robin glanced at David, who gave her a bored shrug. The boy seemed to be beating a hasty retreat behind his accustomed wall of sullenness. But Robin didn't feel any sense of disappointment. It was only natural that he would seesaw back and forth. For two days, his life had followed an unexpected path. It would be unrealistic to expect miracles. Progress could be measured only one step at a time.

Her gaze returned to Eric, and she felt the now familiar tug of attraction toward him. She wanted to be near him, stay near him. Stay *very* near to him. But not a muscle moved. "Lovely," she repeated quietly. "I — I think I'll take a walk."

"Good idea," Eric said. But that wasn't what his eyes said. His eyes asked her not to go, not to move away from him. Not to tear them apart.

Suddenly Robin started. She had no idea how long they'd been standing there, staring at each other, with everyone else moving about them to clear the table. When she looked around, Samantha winked at her, and David was nowhere to be seen.

Robin ducked her head and hurried upstairs for a sweater.

A light fog had rolled in, making it difficult to see the twin pillars of rock at the entrance to the bay. Robin snuggled closer into her sweater, slipping her fingers into the sleeves to protect them from the moist, chilled air. She walked to the end of the pier, then restlessly moved on to the trail leading to the rim of the cliff.

From the top of the cliff, she paused to look behind her. Through the misty veil, she could see the lights that had been switched on early in the houses of Dunnigan Bay, soft yellow beacons that signaled home and safety. Toward the ocean, she could see nothing past a certain point, the white-capped breakers seeming to appear as if by magic.

Robin sighed and kicked a loose stone. What did she do now? What was her next move? From the beginning — when she had first talked to Eric on the telephone, when she had hesitated to take that first step across the inn's threshold, when she had shared in their first shock of mutual aware-ness — she had sensed that everything could easily spiral out of control. Now it had.

Love wasn't something that came easily to her. She couldn't think, "Oh, I love him!" and then forget it. She had thought she might be in love once or twice in her life, but she had always found a reason not to be. Now that it had finally happened, ir-revocably, she wasn't in a position to accept it. Her entire existence here was based on a lie.

And the truth shall make you free! For her,

truth would be the end of everything.

Robin started to walk along the path. At the fork leading down to the beach, she turned back. The fog was getting thicker as the day's light rapidly dimmed, and she didn't want to miss a step.

A form emerged out of the grayness along the path. At first she thought it was Eric, and her heart missed a beat. But as they drew closer to each other, she recognized Benjamin.

"Eric had a panic call from Eileen Clarke, and he had to rush over to Vista Point," Benjamin explained. "He asked me to see that you made it home safely. He said to tell you he didn't want you to pull a Frank Whittaker. That you'd understand what he meant."

Robin laughed even as she felt a rush of pleasure at Eric's thoughtfulness. "He's referring to a guest we had last week. Everyone wanted to chuck him off the cliff."

"Then you definitely don't want to be Frank Whittaker."

"For more than one reason."

"I could make a rather risqué joke about that, but I won't . . . seeing that we've barely met."

"Does that usually stop you?"

"Rarely. But in this instance . . ."

212

He fell into step beside her, following through with Eric's request by choosing the side closer to the cliff's edge for himself.

Robin thought about the heartbroken young boy he had once been and compared him to the fine-looking young man he had become. On the surface, he seemed to be the most satisfactorily adjusted in the family, always good for a laugh. But jokers sometimes hid behind their jokes, presenting a happy front but hurting privately. From her previous conversation with David and her silent observation at dinner, she realized Benjamin was not a man to be easily pigeonholed.

"You're in law school?" she began, for something to say.

"You need a lawyer?" he quipped, but there was a little sting behind the words, as if they were probing more deeply than they first appeared to be.

"Not really, no," she replied, giving an uneasy little laugh.

They continued in silence for several steps.

"You're an excellent cook," he said at last. "That chowder was delicious."

"Thank you."

"Samantha tells me everything you make is delicious."

"Samantha is easy to please."

"So does Barbara, and so does Eric. And Eric isn't easy to please."

Robin searched for a reply. What he'd said seemed more like an accusation than a compliment. "I — I try," she stammered.

"This is an odd place for someone like you," he continued.

"Like me?" she repeated. "Should I be insulted?"

"Only if you want to be. Where have you worked before?"

"A number of places."

"Name one."

"Why?"

"Because I'd like to know."

"In San Francisco?"

"That's a good start."

"Umberto's in the Marina District." She stopped walking. "Would you like to see my references?"

He faced her. "Would you give them to me?"

"If you have serious questions about my abilities, yes."

"It's not your ability I'm questioning," he said quietly.

"Why don't you just say what you mean," Robin suggested flatly. Her heart had started to thump rapidly, and she felt a definite shortness of breath. Though her existence here was based on a lie, a lie she now hated, it was the lie itself that allowed her to function. She had to defend it in order to defend herself. She waited for his reply.

"I don't want to see my brother hurt."

"Neither do I!"

"Are you going to hurt him?"

"I hope not."

"Do you love him?"

Robin resumed walking and Benjamin followed.

"I asked you a question," he said when he'd caught up with her.

"Which I consider extremely rude."

"Lawyers have a reputation for asking rude questions."

"You're not a lawyer . . . yet."

They turned down the path to Dunnigan Bay. At the street, Benjamin caught hold of her arm. Swinging her around to face him, he said, "You have to understand how we all feel about Eric —"

"Don't you think I already know?" she interrupted testily. "It's all I've heard since I arrived here. How after your father died, Eric raised you. How he gave up everything. How hard it was . . . how grateful everyone is. I appreciate that. I'm sure he appreciates that. But I don't need warning off."

"That wasn't what I —"

215

"First Allison. Now you. Who's next? David?"

"Allison?" he repeated.

"She threatened to tear me to shreds!"

Benjamin blinked, then, his humor returning, remarked, "At least I didn't do that."

"Almost as bad! You questioned my integrity."

"All I want is for you to play with a fair hand."

"So you don't care if I love Eric or not?"

"I care . . . because he cares."

"I think you should mind your own business."

"Eric *is* my business."

Robin pulled away from him. "Thanks for coming to walk with me," she said coolly.

"No problem at all. It's been . . . interesting."

She started to walk away.

"I won't be here tomorrow, you know," he called after her. "I'm going back to San Francisco."

"In order to check up on me?" she challenged without looking back.

He laughed. "I go to school, remember? But I just might have dinner at Umberto's. Do you object?"

"No, go ahead. The owner knows me."

"What do you recommend from the menu?"

"The hemlock!"

His laughter at her outrageous answer continued to ring in her ears even as she passed through the gate and started up the walkway to the inn.

Once inside, washed by the same pale yellow light that had shown the way to safety and warmth from the cliff, Robin leaned back against the door and closed her eyes.

She didn't wish Benjamin harm. She didn't wish any of them harm. But no matter which way she turned, she was afraid that it was going to happen. She couldn't even run away. Not for a week, at least. Barbara was relying on her to make the wedding cakes. And David . . . the boy was starting to make progress. If she was simply to vanish, how would that affect him? So many people in his life had just disappeared.

Gifts from friends and relatives were starting to pile up in one corner of the entryway. Festive bows and wrappings. A celebration.

Instead of being happy, Robin felt deeply troubled. What if Benjamin went to Umberto's and Simon, her friend, forgot what he was supposed to say? Weeks had gone by since she'd primed him with her new name and her false story. What if he told Benja-

217

min the truth, and Benjamin came back to Heron's Inn and told everyone else?

Robin couldn't prevent the cry of pain that escaped her lips, and afraid that someone might have heard, she rushed down the hall and out the French doors into the garden.

Walls were too constrictive for the way she felt. She needed room to think, room to try to form a plan . . . room to cry unseen, if she felt the need.

Barbara sighed deeply in the seat next to her brother. Eric glanced away from the road to look at her.

"Are you going to be glad when it's over?" he asked fondly.

"If I'd known it was going to be this bad, I'd have taken Samantha's advice and Timothy and I would have eloped."

"Eileen would never have forgiven you."

"At this point, I'd be willing to take my chances."

"Just think . . . when you're standing at the end of the aisle in your beautiful dress and the church is filled with flowers, the organ starts to play and Timothy is waiting for you . . ."

"And you're at my side, looking handsome in your best tux."

218

"My only tux!" he said with a laugh.

"And we start to walk down the aisle. I'm glad you're going to be with me, Eric. Helping me to get through it. I'm grateful you've been helping me all along. Without you . . ."

"You'd have done just fine."

Barbara shook her head. "Not with Eileen. She knows just how to steamroll over me."

"One day you're going to have to take a stand," he said gently. "You can't let her continue to run your life. If you do, you'll be miserable."

"There was a time when I hoped that you'd take her off our hands."

Eric looked sharply away from the road. "Me?" he said incredulously.

"She'd agree to anything you asked."

"Not that!"

"Particularly that."

Eric started to laugh. "Oh, come on."

Barbara's gaze was steady. "I wish you could be as happy as Timothy and I will be when this is all over."

Eric said nothing, but his thoughts turned back to Robin. She was never out of his mind for long, day or night.

"Eric?" Barbara questioned hesitantly. "You and Robin . . . is something serious going on between the two of you?"

"Possibly."

219

"Do you want there to be?"

"I'd like nothing better."

"What about Robin?"

"That's the big question mark."

"I don't know how she couldn't like you."

"I've already had an earful from Benjamin and Allison. Is it your turn now?"

"What do you mean? I don't understand."

"Aren't you going to tell me I should know a lot more about her? That it's silly and irresponsible for me to think I could love someone I've known for such a short time."

"Which one said that?" she demanded.

"Allison."

"Allison isn't the person to talk about being silly and irresponsible. She married Patrick before any of us got to meet him. And look what happened to them. I *know* Robin. I *like* Robin. So do Samantha and David."

"David especially. It's like she's worked some kind of magic on him."

"I couldn't believe it at dinner tonight when he took up for you and the twins!"

"Me, either. But it felt good."

"Allison is probably only trying to protect you from what happened to her. I can understand that. And Benjamin . . . he's just met her. Give him a little time. But if you love her, Eric, that's enough. You don't have to be concerned about us any longer, what we think about things. It's what you think that matters."

"You're forgetting someone."

"I am? Who?"

"The lady in question."

Barbara smiled one of those secretive smiles that can drive a man crazy. "I wouldn't worry about Robin too much."

"Why? Has she said something to you?"

"No. But I can tell."

"You can tell. What can you tell?"

"That she likes you."

"Then why did you ask me how she felt earlier?" he asked with mild exasperation.

"Because I wanted to see what you'd say."

"Did I raise you to be so devious?" he demanded.

Barbara grinned. "I suppose you did. And you did a good job, too."

Barbara leaned close to rest her head on his shoulder, and Eric reached back to pat her cheek.

He found her in the garden. He came on silent feet and surprised her as she stood staring at a cluster of pink rhododendron blossoms. In the misty light cast into the night through the glass panes of the French doors, the blooms had a pale opalescence that lent them a fairy-tale air. He slipped his arms about her waist, drawing her back against him as he bent to kiss the side of her neck.

For a blissful moment, Robin complied, reveling in the spontaneity of the act. Then, remembering, she resisted.

"I love the way your hair smells," he said softly in her ear.

"Don't," she breathed.

He turned her to face him. "Why not? I love you."

Robin avoided his gaze. "You don't know what you're saying."

"But I do." He leaned sideways for a better view of her face. When he saw the traces of her earlier tears, he stiffened. "You've been crying," he said. "Why?"

What could she answer? *Because everything is so hopeless. Because I love you and now you say you love me, and everything could explode in our faces at any moment. Because almost everything I've told you about myself is false. Because I hurt so badly because of that, and there's absolutely nothing I can do to change it. Because if I do, if I tell you the truth, you'll hate me. I am that little girl on the beach!*

Robin bit her bottom lip. "It's too complicated," she said.

His fingers threaded through the hair at the back of her neck. "I have very strong shoulders," he murmured.

At his gentle offer, moisture again stung her eyes. She allowed her head to fall lightly against his chest.

He gathered her closer, seemingly content for the moment just to hold her. "Whatever the problem is, Robin, I may not be able to solve it, but I can help."

Robin shook her head.

"It can't be that bad," he chided lightly. "You haven't robbed a bank, have you?"

In spite of herself, Robin gave a watery laugh. "No."

"Then?"

When she didn't answer, his chest rose and fell in a deep sigh. Moments later, he said softly, "I meant what I said earlier. I do love you. I didn't expect to, but it happened. I can't change it. If you don't love me yet, I can wait. I'm a very patient man."

She looked up at him. "No. I don't — I do —"

"You do love me?" He hung on her last word.

"I can't say that!"

"Do you feel it?"

"I can't say that, either!"

"You say there isn't anyone else, yet —"

But there *was* someone else. Only not in the way he meant. There was his father.

He lifted her left hand and examined it in the half-light. "You told me before you weren't married. Is that the truth?"

"Yes," she replied tightly, finding solace in being able to admit to that much, at least.

His relief was evident. "Then we'll go on from there. If and when you need my help, I want you to promise to come to me. You don't have to be alone in this, Robin. Whatever it is."

He brought her hand to his lips and with exquisite tenderness kissed each fingertip.

CHAPTER TWELVE

Robin spent the next day trying to forget what had happened the night before.

To complicate matters, as she and Eric had come inside from the garden, Donal Caldwell had arrived back at the inn from the evening he'd spent with friends. His delighted smile upon seeing them hadn't needed interpretation. His wink at her and his aside to Eric, "Is there a possibility of two weddings in the Marshall family this year?" only added to Robin's discomfort.

Eric, of course, had saved the moment with his easy charm. He had humored the older man, while at the same time speeding Robin's departure upstairs. Robin thought Donal a dear, but at that particular moment she had been too emotionally raw to deal with him — or with anyone else, for that matter.

She felt the same way the next morning and, after breakfast, slipped out of the house and into her car. As she left Dunnigan Bay behind, she wondered what it would be like to leave it for the last time.

During the long hours of the night, Robin had made a decision. Shortly after the wedding — if she was allowed to stay that long, if Benjamin didn't come back to expose her — she would break her commitment to stay on for the summer and return to her real life in the Bay Area. It wouldn't be easy, but it had to be done. She would cushion the blow to David as best she could. As far as Eric was concerned . . . Robin shied away from the emotional damage she would inflict on him. If she stayed, it would only be worse.

She could handle her own pain, but she couldn't bear to think of the pain he would suffer when she could neither tell him the truth about herself nor admit her love for him. She would have to build lie upon lie to find a reason why they couldn't be together. He'd said he was a patient man, but he wasn't that patient.

She followed the twisting highway through the isolated beauty of the coastal redwoods. After breaking onto the busy interstate highway, she didn't stop until she arrived in San Francisco.

She had made do with what implements

she could find when preparing the decorations for the test cake. For the actual wedding, she wanted to do it right. She stopped at a supply store she knew and spent the next hour picking and choosing what she needed.

She bought a quick take-out dinner at a corner café and ate her meal while sitting on a bench staring across San Francisco Bay toward her home in the Berkeley hills. She longed to see her apartment again, to just be herself for a half hour — to touch some of her favorite things. But she had one other chore to accomplish before she headed north again. If the idea had occurred to her earlier, she'd have stopped there first. But she only thought of it while she was eating.

Umberto's was busy as usual, the owner and the staff all bouncing back and forth to cater to the hungry customers, but Robin had parked her car in a tow-away zone and could only spare a few moments herself.

She pushed her way through the line of people waiting to be seated, drawing a number of censorious glares. But when Simon looked up to see her and welcomed her with an exuberant embrace, the aggrieved patrons returned to their previously patient wait.

"Has anyone been here asking about me?"

she asked her friend in a rush.

A few minutes later she had jumped back into her car and was zooming off, just as a parking control officer on her three-wheel motorcycle rounded the corner at the end of the street.

That was one problem taken care of, she thought with satisfaction. Benjamin had told her he was coming back to San Francisco today, and he had yet to show up at the restaurant. She had beaten him to it. She had gotten there in time to remind Simon of his promise to cover for her. Now Benjamin could ask all the questions he wanted.

She arrived back at Heron's Inn shortly after one in the morning, and as she made her way upstairs and down the partially lighted hallway, she stepped as quietly as she could. She didn't want to wake anyone.

But as she paused to open Bridget's door, she heard a door farther down the hall softly shut.

Eric's door. He had waited up for her. Had it crossed *his* mind to wonder if she would return?

As Eric had said, the out-of-town guests started to arrive on Thursday morning. By Friday noon, all those who were expected to come were there. Robin was hard-pressed to keep everyone fed. Unlike paying guests, the new arrivals were in a festive mood and wanted to be treated as members of the family, which they either were or would be in a few days' time. David helped her in the kitchen as much as he could and even Samantha pitched in when she was able, but the girl spent most of her time helping Eric, whom everyone seemed to think existed solely to entertain them. Between catering to their needs and having to continue to calm Eileen, Eric was beginning to look a bit stressed.

Barbara fared little better. As the days went by, she seemed to exist more and more on nerve alone. She had another argument with Timothy, which again blew over quickly.

Robin was glad she had spent the first part of the week, when she had had the time, creating all the flowers that she would use on the wedding cake. One entire counter had been placed off-limits to everyone so she could prepare and store the flowers on it.

At six o'clock on Friday evening, as the principal members of the wedding party left for the rehearsal and dinner in Vista Point, Robin closed the kitchen. She'd provided an array of snacks in the dining room, along with enough coffee, tea and soft drinks to keep the guests satisfied.

She drew a bracing breath. She had made the cakes the night before. The next step she considered the most challenging and rewarding.

Hours passed without her being aware of it. Her concentration was so intense that she didn't hear the returning cars or the cheerful voices in the other rooms.

Finally, exhausted, she stepped back to view her work with critical eyes. She saw little to complain about. If pressed, she would have to admit that both the stacked, three-tier wedding cake and the single-sheet chocolate groom's cake were works of art. She had outdone herself.

She drew the back of her hand across her forehead, sweeping aside loose strands of hair. Now she only hoped Barbara and Timothy would like them, and even Eileen. The three-tier cake was very much like the single layer she had shown them previously, only this time the decorations cascaded from tier to tier in a veritable waterfall of flowers. Baby-fine pale pink ribbons and equally delicate pipings of royal icing blended with the palest hint of color in the flowers. The groom's cake was simpler, as she had planned, decorated with chocolate icing and pale pink buttercream rosebuds.

A light tap sounded on the swing door leading into the dining room. Robin jumped slightly, startled. "Come in," she called. She wondered if the guests needed more coffee or tea.

Instead, Eric stepped into the room, holding the door partway open. He looked tired but happy in his fisherman's knit cream-colored sweater and dark slacks. A few new lines had formed around his eyes and deepened in his cheeks. But nature had a way of increasing a man's allure when that happened, she thought ruefully.

"I was wondering if —" he started to say, then caught sight of the wedding cake. He stared at it a long moment before his incredulous gaze came back to her.

She held her breath. She herself thought it was beautiful, but beauty was very much in the eye of the beholder.

"Magnificent!" he decreed. "You actually — I've never seen anything like it."

Robin wiped her hands on the short towel caught in the apron string at her waist. "You really like it?"

He stepped away from the door to examine the cakes more closely. His gaze went from one to the other. "What would something like this cost if it were ordered at a fancy bakery?"

Robin merely shrugged.

"Several hundred dollars, at least," he decided.

More like eight or nine, Robin knew, because of the labor and artistry involved. "I've told you," she said. "It's my present to Barbara and Timothy."

"They're very lucky people."

Once again Robin shrugged.

She glanced away for a moment, and in that moment Eric came to stand next to her. When she looked around, she caught an oddly whimsical look in his eyes.

Her body began a fine vibration, like a deftly struck tuning fork. Being near him always did that to her, from the very first time they'd met.

He licked a finger and touched it to her forehead.

Robin ducked automatically.

He tasted his finger and laughed. "Icing!" he exclaimed.

Robin went to the sink to dampen a fresh towel. "It's all over me," she complained.

He took the towel away from her but, instead of using it, dropped it on the counter. Then he brushed the loose hair away from her forehead and started to kiss the sensitive skin, his tongue making soft forays to remove the sugar.

Robin wanted to melt. She wanted to tell him, "Just a minute . . . let's secure the door, and then we can kiss all night long." But her personal code wouldn't allow her to do that. She could lie to him in one way, but not in another. Not in the most basic, most intimate relationship that existed between a man and a woman. In another week she would be gone from Heron's Inn. She couldn't betray him that deeply, not if she wanted to live with herself later.

She eased away from him, offering a tremulous smile. "Behave yourself," she admonished.

Reluctantly he let her go. Someone laughed on the other side of the door and he glanced around. "I suppose you're right. We wouldn't want to shock the relatives."

"I was surprised you're back so soon. What time is it?" she asked.

"After midnight."

"It's already Barbara's wedding day!"

"She went straight to bed, but I doubt she's going to sleep tonight. She was like that as a kid. Always too excited before a big event to get any rest."

"I was like that, too. I —"

Robin busied herself cleaning a smear

of dried icing off the counter. Right now it hurt to think of herself as a child. Nor did she want to speculate about what it would be like for her as she waited through a night for her own wedding day. It was a waste of time. The groom could never be Eric. Therefore, there would be no marriage.

"Are you almost finished in here?" he asked. "It's late and you've been working hard."

"Just another few minutes," she said, continuing to scrub at the counter. "I won't be long."

She could hear people climbing the stairs and walking around in the rooms above the kitchen. The house seemed to be settling for the night.

He crossed slowly to the door. "Can I do anything?" he asked, pausing.

Robin shook her head. She refused to look at him. If she did, her code might be unable to withstand the onslaught.

The cakes received all kinds of attention the next morning. Robin found a crowd of relatives in the kitchen, oohing and aahing.

"You must be a professional," someone said.

"Beautiful enough for a poem," Aunt Rachel murmured. Aunt Rachel was a much older woman than Robin expected. She was actually the aunt of the Marshalls' late mother. In her early seventies, she got along famously with Donal Caldwell.

Robin accepted their compliments and started breakfast. Halfway through her preparations, Barbara came downstairs. Dark circles were visible beneath her eyes, showing her lack of sleep. Her movements were lethargic. But when she saw the cakes, she broke into a huge smile and ran to examine them more closely.

"Beautiful! Absolutely beautiful!" she repeated, swinging around to kiss Robin's cheek. "I knew everything was going to be all right. The sun is shining . . . the weather forecaster said it's going to be clear all day. My shoes arrived in time. We found another organist. After all the headaches, it truly *is* going to be all right. Oh, thank you, thank you, thank you!"

Robin's head pounded. She'd probably had as little sleep last night as Barbara, but she didn't have Barbara's reason for being in such a good mood. She forced a smile. "I can only claim credit for the cakes."

"They're perfect. Better than perfect. What Eileen wanted to order was nowhere near as nice as this."

Robin allowed herself a small, pleased smile.

David came into the kitchen as Robin straightened up after breakfast. Still clinging to the garb he loved best — his torn jeans and faded T-shirt — he sat down at the narrow table. "I'm getting tired of being nice," he grumbled.

"I know. It *is* a strain," Robin teased him.

David sighed and threaded his fingers through his long blond curls. "The tux is going to be a strain, too."

"You'll look very handsome."

"You think so?"

"I know so." She took the chair across from him.

"I'm also tired of the house being full of all these people. I like the paying customers better."

"Because they pay?"

"Because they don't criticize. I leave them alone, they leave me alone."

"And these people don't?"

"Aw, no! They look at me like I'm some kind of freak, then they give me these little digs, you know. 'Your hair is a little long, isn't it? Where did you get those jeans, the Salvation Army? Doesn't your brother give you money for clothes?' Really funny."

"Maybe they're not sure what to say to you," she suggested.

"I'd rather they say nothing than judge me. They don't even know me. They don't know who I am. Maybe I don't think so much of the way they dress, either."

Eric strode into the room. He didn't look as if his night had gone any better than Robin's. "Any chance of another cup of coffee?" he asked. He noticed David and in a mistaken moment complained, "Weren't you supposed to at least get a trim?"

David swelled up like a toad. He jumped to his feet to face his brother. "It wasn't my idea to be involved in this thing! If my hair's not good enough the way it is, neither am I! I'm *not* going to cut it! Ever!"

"You're going to look funny with it dragging on the floor," Eric shot back.

"It's nowhere near the floor!"

"Give it a few years and it will be."

Robin stood in between them. "Come on, guys," she cajoled, a hand on each male chest. "This isn't the time or place. Everyone's nerves are a little ragged. David, your hair is fine. Eric, let me get you the cup of coffee you asked for. Barbara is already under enough pressure without hearing the two of you argue."

"I'm tired of people making comments

about the way I look," David snarled, but with less force than before.

"By people, don't you mean me?" Eric demanded.

"Everyone."

Eric seemed ready to make another sharp reply, but instead he rubbed the back of his neck and after a moment said, "You're right. My comment was out of line. Forget I said anything."

David's thin face lost more of its hostile expression. He stuffed his hands into his pockets and gave a jerky nod.

Samantha entered the room by way of the back stairs. "Oh, here you are!" she chirped happily. "Eric, Barbara wants to know if you have the key to her suitcase. She thought she had it, but it seems to have disappeared."

Eric frowned. "I haven't seen it."

"Well, she asked me to ask you."

"I'd better talk to her."

"Good idea." She grinned at David. "Are you ready for this?"

"Do I have a choice?"

"I won't ever put you through it, I can promise you that."

"You say that now . . ." David grumbled.

"I'll say it then, too. This is too much like torture!"

Eric started for the back stairs.

"Don't you want your coffee?" Robin asked, interrupting him.

"No, not now. I'd better go see Barbara." The doorbell had rung moments before. Someone must have answered it, because a small woman with a halo of white hair, a round face and a determined expression marched into the kitchen to demand, "What's this I hear about someone holding a wedding today?" Then her face broke into a beaming smile, she dropped her suitcase and opened her arms wide, encouraging an enthusiastic greeting.

"Bridget!" Samantha yelped in joy and surprise before rushing over to her.

"Bridget?" Eric and David said in unison.

The cook extracted herself from Samantha's embrace, patting the young woman's cheek to show her continued love. " 'Tis me. All the way back from the Emerald Isle!"

"But how — I thought —" Samantha stammered.

Bridget beamed again. "My cousin the earl. I told him how badly it was breaking my heart not to be here today, and he surprised me by putting me on his private jet. Can you believe that? The man owns his own jet! So here I am. But tomorrow the jet has to go back, and he made me promise to be on it. With so much time left of Maureen's and my vacation, he's offered us a place to stay in London, if we want to come . . . after we get our fill of seeing Ireland, of course. He's such a nice person, we're going to take him up on it." She looked around. "Where's Barbara? And Benjamin . . . and Allison? And who is this?" She looked at Robin with intense curiosity.

"Barbara's upstairs," Eric said, answering in the same order as her questions. "Benjamin should be here any minute — he couldn't make it any earlier. I have no idea where Allison is. And this is Robin . . . I told you about her in my letter."

"My replacement," Bridget murmured.

"Your *temporary* replacement," Robin corrected. She smiled and held out her hand.

The older woman's grip was strong. She didn't immediately let go. Robin felt as if everything about her were being weighed.

A small frown crinkled Bridget's brow. She had sensed something. "Very nice to meet you," she said formally.

The twins burst into the room, quickly followed by Allison.

"Bridget!" they all cried, demanding the cook's attention.

Robin eased away from the family scene.

Now three people were suspicious of her. She slipped into the garden before making her way to the street.

The breeze off the ocean was bracing, exactly what she needed. She strolled to the pier, sat down for a while, then, after checking her watch, made her way back to the inn. The cakes were to be transferred to the reception hall and Barbara had asked her to accompany them, to be sure that they arrived intact.

Just as she passed through the gate in the picket fence, Benjamin rode up on his motorcycle. The loud roar before he cut the engine caused several birds to take flight.

He secured the stand, doffed his helmet and balanced it on the elongated seat. He made a striking figure in his leathers.

He grinned at her. "Caught in the act! Playing off!" he teased.

"I notice you didn't put in an early appearance."

"I know how to avoid last-minute panics — stay away for as long as you can."

He stood outside the gate, making no effort to enter.

"Bridget's here," Robin said.

"From Ireland?" he questioned blankly.

"She'll tell you all about it. By the way, you'll be happy to know, she doesn't like me, either."

"I never said I didn't like you," he claimed.

"Did you stop by Umberto's?" She had to know.

"No."

"Why not?"

"I decided to trust you."

He couldn't have hurt her more if he'd thrust a knife into a vital organ. She caught hold of her bottom lip and looked away.

"I thought that would make you happy," he said, frowning.

"I'm ecstatic," Robin murmured.

The front door opened and Samantha leaned out. "Benjamin! Come see who's here! You'll *never* guess!"

"In a minute." He continued to gaze at Robin while Samantha waited. "If you are in some kind of trouble, I do know several lawyers I can recommend."

She shook her head, fighting to keep tears from forming. "It's not that," she said tightly.

"Benjamin!" Samantha repeated, growing impatient.

"Go on," Robin urged him. "Everyone's waiting. I'm just . . . tired. It's been rather hectic here this last week."

Concern still dominated his expression, but he agreed to do as she suggested. "We'll talk later," he said. As he moved past her, Robin reached out to stop him momentarily. "Benjamin? Thanks."

"What for?" he asked, puzzled.

"Just . . . thanks. Now, go on."

She stayed at the gate until the van to transport the cakes pulled up.

By directing her thoughts to her supervisory duties and after a change of scene to Vista Point, Robin was able to pull herself back together in the hour and a half that followed. From this point, she would take her continued stay in Dunnigan Bay one day at a time. The day her instinct told her it was best to leave, she would leave.

The wedding was something of a blur for Eric. Barbara was a radiant bride, Timothy the typical nervous groom. Eileen cried quietly throughout the ceremony and he steeled himself for the even more copious tears he knew she would cry on his shoulder later. David behaved civilly and, he had to admit, cleaned up to look quite handsome in his tux. He wore his hair slicked back in a ponytail and had even accepted a boutonniere to wear in his lapel.

Several times during the ceremony, Eric's gaze had been drawn to Robin, seated a few benches behind the family. Seeing her sad look, he felt fiercely protective. Who was responsible for her hurt? For making her react the way she did? She looked so small, so despondent, so helpless to change whatever it was that was haunting her. He was sure now that it was a man. And if he ever gained a hint as to who the man was . . .

Unreasoning jealousy washed over him. He wanted to strike out, to gain some kind of physical release. But he was at his sister's wedding. With an effort of will, he brought himself back to the happiness of the day.

He lost track of Robin at the reception. There were an inordinate number of hands to shake and cheeks to kiss. Friends and neighbors enjoyed the champagne and devoured Robin's cakes. Eileen had to be consoled. There were photographs to be staged and miles of video to be shot.

When it was all over — after Barbara and Timothy had run out of the reception hall under a barrage of rice to catch a plane for their one-week honeymoon in Hawaii — he sank into a chair, leaned his head back and closed his eyes. He was tired.

"Eric?" He heard Samantha's voice. She sat down in the chair beside him and leaned her head against his shoulder.

"Quite a day, hmm?" he murmured, lifting his head slightly.

"Barbara was happy."

"Which makes it worthwhile."

"I'm still glad it's over."

Eric chuckled tiredly in agreement. He didn't need to put his relief into words.

Samantha sat up and smoothed the skirt of her blue gown. "I wonder if I'll ever wear this dress again."

"Not many places to wear it up here," he said.

She was quiet. "I hadn't planned to mention this now. Maybe I still shouldn't."

"What?" He sensed what was coming.

"In the fall, I think I'd like to move back to San Francisco."

"On your own?"

"With a couple of friends. We'd share an apartment."

"What will you do for a job?"

"I'll find one."

"That might not be easy."

"Are you trying to talk me out of it?"

"You're old enough to make your own decisions."

Samantha stared down at her hands. "I should have waited until later to tell you." She looked as miserable as Robin had earlier.

"If it's what you want," Eric said after several seconds had passed, "then do it."

245

Her face brightened, then fell. "But what about you? Who will help you with the inn? Barbara's gone, I'll be gone. What will you do? You can't manage it all on your own, can you?"

"I'll do what I've always planned to do someday — hire help."

"I won't go!" she cried, changing her mind. "I'll stay with you."

"Forever?" he teased.

She pulled a face. "I know," she said brightly. "You could always marry Robin."

"I'd still have to hire extra help. Do you think she'd want to start cleaning floors and bathrooms? 'Marry me, my dear, and I'll shower you with bottles of cleaning fluid.' That doesn't sound very romantic."

Samantha giggled. "Yes, but you'd be happy. And I wouldn't have to worry about you anymore."

"I've told you before, stop worrying about me. I can take care of myself."

"Don't you *want* to ask Robin to marry you?"

Samantha was so completely different from Allison. She took people as they were. She wasn't afraid of them, or suspicious. On the other hand, once Allison had figured out what she wanted from life, she had gone after it with a single-minded ferocity and not looked back to question herself. Would the girls' lives have been different if their father had lived? Was it something that he, Eric, had done or not done as he raised them that caused Allison to be so hard-edged and Samantha so willing to trust? And Barbara . . . He hoped with everything that was in him that she would be happy in her marriage.

As time went by, it was getting harder to keep making excuses about why he wasn't pressing his suit with Robin. "Asking someone to marry you isn't always such an easy thing to do," he said in response to her question.

Samantha laughed. "It's like in that Lauren Bacall and Humphrey Bogart movie. You just put your lips together and blow. Only in this case, what you have to do is pry your lips apart and ask. I'm positive she loves you."

"Then why does something keep getting in the way? You wouldn't have any idea what it is, would you? She hasn't confided in you?"

Samantha shook her head.

"Have you seen her lately?" he asked, looking around.

"I thought you knew. She went home with Donal shortly after the cake was cut."

247

Eric pulled on one end of his bow tie to release it. Then he loosened the top buttons of his dress shirt.

"What are you doing?" Samantha asked, eyes twinkling. "Getting ready to change into your superhero suit so you can fly off to the inn to find her?"

Eric's smile was wry. "A superhero I'm not."

"I've always thought you were," she said simply, and in so doing warmed his heart.

CHAPTER THIRTEEN

Robin was in bed when she heard people start to converge on the inn. The party continued for many of the guests, but she didn't get up to join them. No one had asked her to prepare anything or to be on duty in the kitchen, so what they did was their affair. Her headache, which had never truly gone away since that morning, had returned with a vengeance during the reception. It hurt so badly that she had felt nauseated. She still did.

A half-hour later, Robin dragged herself to the bathroom. She was digging in the medicine cabinet when Bridget passed by in the hall. The woman did a double take and stopped.

"Are you feeling unwell?" she asked.

"Fairly unwell," Robin answered tightly.

"What do you need?" the woman asked briskly. She shooed Robin away from the cabinet and installed herself there instead.

"An Alka-Seltzer?" Robin murmured.

Bridget searched through the bits and pieces on the layers of shelves. "Ah!" she said at last. She pulled a paper cup from the decorative dispenser beside the sink and dropped a tablet into the water she'd drawn. It began to fizz immediately. "Drink this," she directed. Robin did. "Do you want another?" she asked.

Robin shook her head. "No, this is fine," she said weakly.

"Too much champagne?" the woman asked brusquely.

Robin looked at her. "Too much tension," she said.

"Let's get you to bed," Bridget decided, taking hold of Robin's arm.

Robin defended her apparent weakness. "I almost never have headaches like this."

"Which room are you in?" Bridget asked.

"Yours," Robin murmured. She'd wanted to ask before she used it that night, but when she'd arrived home so much earlier than everyone else, there was no one to ask. "Eric put me in there, because when the inn is full and Benjamin and Allison and the twins come, there isn't room anywhere else." She paused. "I hope you don't mind."

"Why would I mind? It's a practical solution."

"But where will you sleep tonight?"

Bridget smiled at her for the first time. "I see what Eric means, you are considerate." She assisted Robin to the bed and waited while she slid her legs under the cover. "Don't you worry about me," she assured her. "I'll find a spot. Are Allison and the twins in her old room?" She busied her hands with straightening the quilt.

"They're downstairs."

"Then I could have that room, or I could sleep in Barbara's room. She's not going to need it tonight or any other night for some time to come, I'm sure."

As the woman continued to fuss with the quilt, Robin closed her eyes. The tablet was starting to work. If she could just lie still for a while . . .

She became aware of someone watching her. Her eyes fluttered open. She must have dozed off, she realized.

Bridget nodded. "That's better," she said, satisfied.

Robin attempted to sit up, but Bridget stopped her. "No, no, no!" she repeated. "I just came in to check on you. I didn't mean to wake you."

The headache was gone, and so was the nausea. "I'm much better." Robin copied the older woman's hushed speaking voice.

She had no idea what time it was, but it felt late. She checked the clock on the bedside table. It was after two.

"Eric came by to see you about an hour ago," Bridget said. "I sent him to his own bed."

It took a moment for what the woman had intimated to sink in. "But we don't —"

"None of my business if you do. You're both adults." She paused, cocking her head. "I was curious about you. Eric's letter didn't say a lot, but Samantha's certainly did. I wasn't sure at first, but I watched you at the wedding. I liked what I saw, if that makes any difference to you."

Robin blinked.

When she made no reply, Bridget continued, "I'll most likely be gone by the time you wake up tomorrow morning, so I'll say my goodbyes now and ask that you keep taking good care of my family."

Robin searched for an answer. She felt sure Bridget would know if she lied.

Bridget marched to the door. She didn't pause before going into the hall. She had said what she meant to say, and that was that.

Robin relaxed back into the pillow.

Eric had come to see her.

Considering everything, it was probably a

good idea that she had had an Irish dragon standing guard at her door.

Just as she had announced to Robin, Bridget had departed by the time Robin made her way to the kitchen the next morning. So, too, had a number of the other guests. The two or three who remained were gathering their things in preparation for leaving.

"I slept in. I'm sorry," she apologized to Benjamin and Eric, who were reading the Sunday newspaper and drinking cups of coffee in the dining room. "My alarm didn't ring."

Eric looked at her over the sports section. "I asked Bridget last night to shut it off."

"But —" she began, looking around.

"We took care of everything. No one wanted breakfast, only coffee."

"Hot, *strong* coffee," Benjamin amended.

Robin started for the kitchen. "Don't go in there," Eric said sharply.

She looked at him, confused.

"You're not going to like what you see. The place was left a bit of a wreck last night. Glasses and plates all over. Someone also decided to make a midnight snack. Benjamin and I picked up all the clutter elsewhere, but we needed a cup of coffee before we started cleaning the kitchen."

"How bad *is* it?" she asked.

Eric pushed out a chair with his foot. "Have a cup of coffee."

Robin sat down, but she refused his offer. "That bad?" she asked quietly.

"Let's just say whoever put the snack together managed to get more melted cheese on the floor than they got on any of the crackers."

Robin groaned and covered her face.

Eric pulled one hand away. "Are you feeling better? Bridget said you were ill."

"I *was* better," she answered truthfully.

"Benjamin and I are going to take care of the kitchen. It's been our plan all along."

"That's right," Benjamin confirmed.

The brothers stood up. "Stay here," Eric ordered when Robin tried to rise, as well. "Relax, read the newspaper. We'll be through in half an hour. Then the kitchen is yours again."

The telephone rang, drawing Eric's attention. When he went to answer it, Benjamin slid into his chair.

"I'd planned to spend most of the day here," he said in a low voice, as if he didn't want to be overheard. "But something's come up. I'm sorry we didn't get to have our talk. I meant what I said, though. If ever

you should need the name of a good lawyer
—"

"I'll call *you*," Robin interrupted him. She covered his hand with both of hers. "You're a very nice person, Benjamin. You come from a wonderful family. I won't forget you."

Instead of tempering his concern, her words caused alarm. "Are you leaving? Is that —"

Eric walked back into the room. When he noticed their proximity, his first reaction was to freeze. Then, lifting a brow, he asked with heavy irony, "Am I interrupting something?"

Robin withdrew her hands and Benjamin's cheeks grew ruddy. "Nothing at all," Robin said. "I was just telling Benjamin goodbye."

"Goodbye?" Eric repeated.

"He's leaving soon."

Eric frowned slightly, not completely mollified. His gaze swept over his brother's face before returning to Robin. He fought his jealousy and in the end won. Tapping his brother on the shoulder, he said, "Come on. Let's attack the mess."

Benjamin rose slowly. He glanced at Robin, looked as if he wanted to say something more, then seemed to think better of it. "Sure. Yeah. Let's do it," he said instead.

His hesitation didn't go unnoticed by Eric.

■ ■ ■

By midafternoon all the out-of-town guests had finally departed, Aunt Rachel included. She exchanged home addresses with Donal Caldwell and, after a series of slightly distracted kisses to the remaining nieces and nephews, hopped in her dusty old Plymouth and started back to Idaho.

"Should she be driving that far?" Samantha murmured as they watched her pull away.

"She got here in one piece," Eric reminded her.

"But she seems so . . ."

Eric dropped an arm across his sister's shoulder and started to walk with her along the path to the house. "She's been that way all her life, and she's made it to seventy-three."

His eyes settled on Robin, who walked with David a number of steps ahead. She laughed at something he said, then stuck out her tongue in merry defiance.

It irritated Eric that she could behave so easily with the other male members of his family but be so contained with him. It still rankled when he remembered the way she'd held Benjamin's hand that morning.

Samantha tugged on his sleeve. "I asked if you thought we should call her tomorrow, just to make sure she arrived safely."

Eric stared at her blankly.

"Aunt Rachel," Samantha repeated tersely. "Driving to Idaho. Do you think we should call her tomorrow?"

"Oh . . . yes. Sure. Why not?"

Samantha sighed. "Sometimes lately, talking to you is like trying to talk to a wall. You don't hear half of what I say."

Eric chuckled. "Yes, Mother."

Samantha thumped him on the arm. Then she nodded toward Robin. "Have you asked her?"

"It hasn't been twenty-four hours yet. Give me time!"

"Remember, just pry your lips apart and —"

In a flash, Eric had gripped her in a loose headlock. When he pretended to tighten his hold, she squealed in protest, and he let go.

"I'm going to report you for sister abuse!" she threatened him, laughing as she fluffed her hair back into place.

"The courts would consider it justifiable," he retorted.

Robin looked around. Her gaze settled on him.

Eric felt his body respond. He wanted to

run up there, drag David away from her and kiss her with all his heart. But the best he could do now was smile tightly and nod.

Eric wouldn't hear of Robin preparing dinner that evening. They were all so exhausted, he said, no one should work any more that day. He drove to Vista Point, picked up some fast food — fried chicken, mashed potatoes, gravy, coleslaw, biscuits . . . the works — and brought it home to Heron's Inn.

The cleanup after the meal was minimal, but David hung around the kitchen, helping here and there, mostly seeming to get in the way. Eric sent him several "get lost" glances, but the boy was impervious.

Finally, impatiently, Eric came directly to the point. "Don't you have something to do?" he demanded.

David looked at him, and Eric had to admit that the changes so recently wrought on the young man had gone deeper than he'd thought. Instead of talking back, as he once would have done, David stared at him with a gaze that was steadier, more confident.

"No," he replied. He glanced at Robin. She bent to plug in the coffeemaker and didn't notice.

Eric followed his gaze. He wanted to be alone with her. He switched his attention back to David. "How's the French coming?"

"*Pas mal du tout,*" David answered.

"That's great," Eric said ironically, not understanding any of what he'd said.

Robin straightened. "Not too bad," she translated. Then she said something in what sounded like perfectly accented French herself.

David grinned. "I caught only part of it — something about a student? Hey, you sound like Mrs. Wilson. Why didn't you say you spoke French?"

"No one ever asked."

"Where did you learn to speak it so well?"

"I spent a little time in France, actually," she admitted, glancing uncomfortably at Eric.

Eric shifted. Something else he didn't know about her. Something she'd had no trouble admitting to David. "How long?" he asked.

Her expression tightened, an action someone else might not notice, but as sensitive as he was to her, he caught it right away. His frustration grew.

She shrugged, not bothering to answer in words.

Eric saw the tiny smile that tugged at his

259

brother's lips, and to him it looked like a smirk. He'd had enough of them thrown his way by the boy. He considered himself an expert.

"What are you laughing at?" he demanded, bristling.

"You," David replied.

Everything would have been all right if he hadn't said that. Everyone was tired. Everyone's nerves were stretched after the final days leading up to the wedding, not to mention the wedding itself.

"David," Robin warned, reaching for his arm.

He shook her off. "What's the matter, Eric? Can't you take a joke? Can't the big man stand it when he can't get what he wants?"

Eric glared at him, then he tried to dampen his flash of anger. "Maybe we'd better save this for another day."

"Why?" the boy demanded. "Why should I disappear because you want Robin all to yourself? Maybe I want to be with her, too. Maybe *you* should be the one to leave. Let's ask Robin. Robin, which one? Which one of us do you find it easier to talk with?"

"David," she said, looking strained. "I won't allow you to —"

"That's a rotten thing to do to a person,"

Eric said coldly.

"Oh, but it's right in character for me, isn't it?" David turned away from his brother. "I tried, Robin. I really tried. You saw me! I even wore that stupid suit! But does he appreciate it? No!"

"David, don't," she urged him. Her gaze went to Eric, pleading with him to continue to be patient with his brother. "You appreciated David's efforts, didn't you, Eric?"

"Yes," he replied shortly, meaning it but unable to express it in any other way.

David laughed hollowly. "Yeah, right. I believe that!"

"We're all tired." Robin tried again. "Tomorrow, none of this will —"

"Tomorrow! And the next day and the next!" David interrupted, looking pained. "It doesn't make any difference. A person can't run away from their birthright."

"What are you talking about?" Eric demanded, frowning.

Samantha had heard the raised voices and slipped silently into the room. Seconds later Allison appeared, grumbling irritably about having to send the children outside because she hadn't wanted them exposed to an argument. She stopped when she sensed the potential seriousness of the confrontation.

David looked at them all as if they were

lining up against him, as if he considered Robin his only ally.

"What birthright?" Eric repeated.

"Mine! Yours!" the boy shot back. "The entire Marshall family!"

Eric shook his head. "I don't understand what you're talking about."

"What happened shortly after I was born?" David demanded.

"Mother died," Samantha whispered.

"Exactly!"

"So?" Allison challenged him, frowning fiercely. "That happened a long time ago, Davey. Eighteen years."

"It's been sixteen years since our dad died. Has anyone forgotten that? Eric certainly hasn't. He blames the girl. At least, he says he blames the girl. That's what he's told me all these years." He turned toward Eric. "But it's more than that, isn't it, Eric? It's more than that for all of you!"

Allison moved her head from side to side, while Samantha lifted a hand to cover her mouth. Tears shimmered in the younger woman's eyes. "David, don't," she pleaded huskily.

"Why not? Maybe for once, before I leave, it will be good to get things out in the air."

"Before you leave?" Samantha echoed. "I thought . . . things seemed to be getting so

262

much better."

David snorted, waving a hand in impatient denial.

"Let's hear what he has to say," Eric commanded.

"The Mighty One has spoken," David said sarcastically.

Eric didn't move.

"Don't you think I know you all blame *me?*" David questioned rawly. "Your mother died because of me . . . the aneurysm . . . If I hadn't been born, maybe she'd still be alive. Then you, Eric, wouldn't have had to give up so much of your life . . . good old Saint Eric! I'm *sick* of hearing the stories! And Allison and Barbara and Samantha and Benjamin . . . all of you would have had your mother to see you through the bad times, maybe even prevent them! Instead, you had *me!*"

"I blame the girl, not you!" Eric said tightly. He wondered why Robin seemed to shrink further back into the corner she'd chosen for protection. But he didn't have time to dwell upon it. "And she was your mother, too! Don't talk about her as if she's some kind of stranger."

"She might as well be," David snapped.

"Has anyone ever *once* told you that you were responsible for anything that happened?" Eric demanded. "Me? Any of us?"

"Actions speak louder than words. Or have you never heard that?"

"That's not true!" Allison defended them all. "We've never said anything, done anything . . . because it's not the way we feel. You've seen things that weren't there, Davey."

"Stop calling me that!" he shouted angrily. "My name is David . . . David!"

Allison shook her head in disbelief, still focusing on what her brother had said previously. "Just not there!" she stressed.

"I remember things, Allison. I remember the anger . . . the tears."

"Well of course! I'd just lost my mother! I loved her!"

"Not then, later. I'm not talking about when I was an infant."

"We'd just lost Dad, then!"

"Later than that."

Allison's tough exterior cracked. Tears started to stream down her face. "All right! So I wasn't perfect! I had problems, too, Davey. Maybe I . . . maybe I took some of it out on you over the years. But I wasn't *blaming* you."

"Not just you," he answered quietly, his gaze moving to Samantha.

"Me?" Samantha squeaked. "What did I

ever —"

Eric stepped into the fray. "Leave your sisters out of this. It's really between the two of us. If you have an argument with the way I raised you, David, blame me, not them."

David's smile held a poisonous edge. "Don't you know? I'm an equal opportunity blamer. I blame everyone."

"Everyone but yourself."

That reply wiped the smile from the boy's face. He stared at Eric, then started to circle him. "I'm tired of feeling like a liability. Mom died because of me. Dad — I don't know how — but it had to have been because of me. We moved here because of me. Everything wrong that's happened to this family is because of *me*."

Eric pivoted, slowly following his brother's path. "All along, I only did what I thought was best for you."

"It wasn't enough!"

Eric's jaw tightened. "What do you want to do, Davey? Hit me? Will that make you feel better? Come on." He beckoned with the tips of his fingers. "I can take it."

"No!" Samantha cried. She had heard enough. She threw herself in between her two brothers. "David . . . Eric . . . don't do this! Please! *Please!* Fighting isn't going to solve anything." She grabbed David's raised fist.

David reacted instinctively. He brushed her away with more force than he meant. She recoiled, lost her balance and crumpled onto the floor with a pain-filled cry.

Everyone reacted with shocked silence. Robin broke ranks first and ran to Samantha's side. The girl whimpered but was uninjured. She raised her tearful gaze to David, a mute question in her eyes. Robin gazed at him, as well.

The boy looked horrified by what he'd done. "I didn't — I didn't mean —" he stammered hoarsely. Tears clogged his throat, then flooded his eyes.

Eric stared at him. Without saying a word, he stepped over to Samantha, lifted her into his arms and carried her along the hall and up the stairs to the family's quarters.

Allison wiped angrily at her cheeks, trying to erase all evidence of tears. "That was inexcusable," she said tightly. "You say we hurt you, but there's been many a time that you've hurt us. We worry about you, Davey, because we love you!"

Fresh tears formed in her eyes, and she spun out of the room before they could fall. Her feet thumped heavily on the narrow steps as she ran up the rear stairs.

Robin and David were left alone in the room. Robin got slowly to her feet.

The boy seemed stunned. A single tear escaped his eye, then another and another. "I didn't mean to do it," he whispered.

Robin crossed over to him. She wrapped him in an embrace. The entire scene had been a horrible nightmare. To witness the angry actions, to hear the painful exchanges . . . she'd felt as if she were being torn apart. If she could have gotten a word past her frozen lips, she would have cried out that it wasn't anyone's fault. Not anyone in this family. That if they needed someone to attack, they should attack her. She was the person who had started it all, even though she had had no inkling when she'd been a young girl playing on the beach. Like a pebble dropped into a still pond, the ripples had reverberated through all the years. How much longer would they continue to rip at the fabric of this family? How much longer would the Marshalls and she have to pay the dreadful price?

The boy's thin shoulders shook in remorse and in misery. She held him tightly, as a mother might an injured child, offering what comfort she could.

When he had collected himself enough to pull away, he breathed a broken "Thanks," and with face averted hurried out the French doors. Robin watched him as he darted past the window in the direction of the street.

She felt limp, unnerved to the point where her nerves could feel no more. So when the fluttering began in the corner of the kitchen, near the stove, she didn't jump or start or think to run away. She merely watched it, an unexplained disturbance of the air. A servant girl? The guilty conscience of Micha Talbot? Or . . . Robin caught her breath as an idea occurred to her. Could the ghost be the spirit of Martin Marshall, come to keep a watchful eye on his family?

The tiny hairs on her arms and the back of her neck lifted, while the air continued to quiver and shift.

"Mr. Marshall?" she questioned softly, in a voice reminiscent of herself as a little girl.

The air continued to dance, then abruptly stopped.

Robin caught her bottom lip between her teeth and looked away. If it had been Martin Marshall, paying a watchful visit to his family, he must not have enjoyed what he'd seen.

Did he want her to do something to make amends? Is that why she was the only person outside of Bridget ever to see the phenomenon?

But she *had* tried. She'd done everything she possibly could. There was nothing left for her to do except get away before she hurt them even more.

Besides, as Eric continued to maintain, there wasn't any such thing as ghosts. She was being fanciful, escaping from a difficult reality into the realm of imagination.

Once again, she thought she saw a slight fluttering in the air beside the stove, but it was gone in a second. She drew an unsteady breath, turned her back and walked away.

CHAPTER FOURTEEN

Robin tapped lightly on the door. She'd already looked in on Samantha and found her asleep. In the hour that had gone by since the argument, Allison had gathered the children and taken them for a car ride and had not yet returned. David was nowhere to be seen, and Eric had holed up in his room. It was outside his door that she waited.

The door opened partway. He stood very straight and tall on the other side.

"I'd like to speak with you, please," she requested.

"What about?" he asked tautly. "Could it wait until morning?"

Robin shook her head. "No."

His lips tightened, but he opened the door wider. "If we talk, we do it in here. I've had enough of family conferences." He laughed shortly. "I suppose you have, too, and we're not even your family."

Robin moved inside the room. This was the first time she had been in a space that was solely his, that reflected his tastes, his interests. Comfortably masculine was the tone she supposed the room achieved. It was filled with a double bed, a massive oak wardrobe, a desk and chair, a computer, stacks of account books and papers, an old-fashioned reading lamp and a painting of Dunnigan Bay that must have been fashioned by Donal Caldwell. It had his signature touches of color and style.

Eric watched her silently as she glanced from one object to another. She'd been hesitant to come here — she hadn't wanted him to get the wrong idea. But from the stiff way he'd reacted, she needn't have worried.

She turned to face him. "I've come to talk about David," she announced without preamble.

"Somehow that doesn't surprise me."

She motioned to the desk chair. "May I sit down?"

"Of course."

She perched on the edge of the chair seat. "You, too?" she asked, glancing at the dark striped comforter on his bed. When he declined, she drew a deep breath.

But before she could begin, he said, "Did

271

he ask you to speak with me?"

"No, I'm here on my own. What happened was an accident, Eric. He didn't mean for Samantha to fall. It just . . . happened."

"I'm aware of that."

Robin frowned. "You are?"

His smile was tight. "I think I know my brother a little better than you do."

"Well, yes, but —"

"Samantha knows it, too. She doesn't blame him. She mostly feels sorry that it got to that point."

"We all feel that way," Robin replied.

"Why should it make a difference to you?" he asked starkly.

Robin blinked. "Because I was there! And because . . . I care."

"About David?"

"Well, yes."

"About Samantha?"

"Yes."

"About me?"

Robin shot to her feet. "I didn't come here to talk about us."

"Maybe that's what I want to talk about."

She walked quickly to the door, but he was there ahead of her. He used his body to block her from reaching the doorknob.

She warned him, "If you let this night end without talking to David, he may not be

272

here in the morning."

"I'm aware of that, as well."

"Then . . . are you going to talk to him?"

"Yes."

"Good. Now, let me open the door. That's all I have to say."

"I'd like an answer to my earlier question."

"Which earlier question? You've asked several."

"What are you hiding from, Robin? *Who* are you hiding from?"

"I'm not hiding from anyone!"

"Then why are you being so secretive? Or are you secretive only with me?"

"I don't know what you're talking about."

"You talk freely to David, you talk freely to Benjamin. But with me, you barely say a word."

She turned away, presenting her back. He pulled her against him, burrowing his face into her neck. "It's driving me crazy, Robin. I see you with the others and —"

"I'm no different with the others than I am with you."

"You'd better be!"

She shook her head, denying the misunderstanding. "Not that way. I didn't mean —"

He moved against her, filling her senses.

"I want you, Robin," he breathed huskily. "I want you to be my wife. We can keep the inn, we can sell it. It doesn't matter to me, just as long as we're together."

"No!" she cried brokenly.

He twirled her around to face him. "Why not?" he demanded. "If you say you don't love me, I could deal with that. Say it, if that's what it is. Say it."

All she could do was look at him.

He closed his eyes and drew a ragged breath. "You're not making this very easy, Robin."

She came as close to the truth as she dared. "Sometimes things from the past . . . get in the way of what might be between two people."

"Another man," he said quickly. "I don't care about another man. As long as you don't still love him."

She stood on tiptoe to kiss him. If this was goodbye . . . It was readily apparent now how badly she was hurting him and would continue to hurt him if she allowed things to continue as they were. He would be angry, he wouldn't understand. But she had no other option.

The kiss continued for longer than Robin intended. She came alive to the hard, demanding pressure of his lips, the sweet fire of his touch, the feel of his taut body straining to meet hers.

The kiss finally broke, but not the embrace. He took a step toward the bed.

"No!" She resisted. "No, I can't!"

The seriousness of her resolution penetrated his consciousness. "This isn't some kind of game, you know," he said, halting.

"I know." She tried to keep her voice from trembling.

"I love you, Robin. I want to marry you."

"I know that, too."

"But?" His features hardened. "Do you have some kind of communicable disease? Is that it?"

"No!" she cried.

He dragged a hand through his hair.

Robin wanted to cry. She shouldn't have let things get so far out of hand. She couldn't blame him for being angry. If their positions were reversed, she'd be angry, too.

She put some space between them. "I — I think I should go," she murmured shakily.

He slipped back into his sardonic mood, which was, if anything, darker than before. "Sure. Why not?" He shrugged. "Since you have nothing more to accomplish here."

Robin didn't want to leave him like that. But then, maybe it was best this way. When the time came in the next few days for her to leave Heron's Inn for good, he wouldn't be wondering about the cause. His conclusion would be incorrect, but at least he wouldn't condemn himself.

Her gaze moved over him. This was one of the ways she would remember him best. Strong in body and in mind. Angry, yet not acting on that anger. Wanting her, yet holding back, because it was what she had told him she wanted.

She turned away and quietly let herself out the door.

After the door closed behind her, Eric wanted to yell in frustration. She loved him. He *knew* she loved him. Yet he couldn't get her to say it. What would it take? What else could he do?

He smashed a fist on the desk, making the reading lamp jiggle. He had to find a way. How could they go on as they were, in such a tortured limbo? From this point onward, it was either full speed ahead or full stop. And he couldn't imagine pulling back.

Seconds passed as he remained very still. Then he drew a deep, steadying breath and released it. Problems seldom came in single doses. If he'd learned nothing else raising his siblings, he'd learned that. The most immediate concern tonight was the need to deal with David. After doing that, he would, if necessary, spend the rest of the night reviewing his options with regard to Robin.

The hall was deserted when Eric stepped outside his door. No one moved about the house. In the half light thrown by the lamp still on in the family room, his shadow loomed large as he made his way to David's bedroom. The boy wasn't there. Eric looked inside when there was no answer to his knock, and all that greeted him were walls plastered with rock posters, a heap of discarded clothing, and CD cases spread all over the floor.

He was just pulling the door shut when David turned into the hall and saw him. A mixture of emotions passed over the boy's face, mostly guilt and indignation. His thin body stiffened.

"Aren't I allowed *any* privacy?" he demanded, stepping past Eric to belatedly block the doorway.

"We need to talk," Eric said quietly.

"We've already talked." David's words were clipped.

"In private," Eric insisted. "May I come in?"

"You've already been in."

"Looked in. There's a difference."

"I don't see what we have left to talk about," David grumbled contentiously.

"Please."

The simple request, after everything that had come earlier, seemed to startle the boy. Without uttering another word, he opened the door.

Eric stepped inside. David kicked some clothes out of the way, removed a stack of books from a chair and offered him a seat.

David didn't take a seat himself, preferring instead to remain mobile. "So?" he asked after an uneasy moment had passed. "What's left to say?"

"Just that you've got a few things wrong about Mom's death. The doctor said the aneurysm was probably there, hidden, for a number of years. It could have given way at any time during or after any one of her pregnancies. If they'd known, she would have been advised not to have children. Then none of us would be here."

"Why didn't you tell me this before?"

"I never knew you were curious."

"I'd call it more than curious!"

Eric didn't rise to the challenge. "Still," he said steadily, "I never knew."

David's frown was intense as he mulled over what his brother had just told him.

"As for Dad," Eric continued, "how could

you have been responsible? You were only two. A two-year-old child isn't capable of causing anyone's death."

"You blame the girl."

"She was older. She put herself at risk."

"Do you think she wanted to die? Do you think Dad wanted to die?"

Eric stood up. "I didn't come here to talk about what I think."

"Well, maybe we should. Maybe we just should! You're not always so right about everything, Eric, even though you seem to think you are!"

"I never claim to be right all the time."

"Think about it. If one of us has an idea and you have a different one, whose idea do we follow? If one of us wants to do this or that and you don't think we should, do we ever get to do it?"

"It makes a difference how old you are. You're still a kid, David. I did the same thing with the others when they were your age."

"I'm eighteen! I'm old enough to be out on my own. To be free of you and all the others."

"Is that what you want?" Eric asked.

"Yes!" David's answer was forceful, then he recanted almost immediately, saying miserably, "No."

Eric hesitated before placing a hand on the boy's shoulder. David didn't jerk away.

"It may not seem like it sometimes," Eric said, "but we do love you." Then, before the boy could reassert his independence, Eric let his hand drop away.

Many words had been left unsaid as Eric walked to the door. He wanted to advise David to give himself some time, to think about what he wanted and not do anything rash, not to leave before they'd had an opportunity to discuss the situation calmly. But if he said any of those things, David might take it that he was issuing another order. Trying to tell him what to do . . . again.

He was almost into the hall when David called after him. "Sam . . . she's all right, isn't she? She's not hurt?"

"She's fine," Eric answered.

David nodded and closed the door.

As Eric moved back down the hall to his room, he had no real reason to expect that the situation was going to improve between him and David, but for the first time in many months — years, even — he felt hopeful.

No light shone from beneath the door of Robin's room. Either she was already asleep or she was in bed staring at the ceiling

280

through the darkness, just as he planned to do in a very short time.

Everyone in the household was more subdued than usual the next morning, but as David had angrily suggested, clearing the air might have done some good. Even though nothing had been resolved, a careful observer would notice that small changes had occurred.

Allison seemed somewhat less brittle as she pitched in to help the others prepare the inn for the next day's scheduled guests, her attitude toward Robin included. She seemed less inclined to look upon her as an outsider, slightly less suspicious.

David was quiet and thoughtful, while Eric seemed to go out of his way to be more tolerant of his youngest brother.

Samantha, reacting to the changes in the others, resumed her happy outlook on life, but with less strain, less fear that at any moment a volcano of emotions might erupt.

It was Eric's behavior that puzzled Robin the most. He was friendly and polite to her, but not insistent. Last night might not have happened. He made no reference to it, either overtly or covertly. Robin knew he still cared for her, but it was clear that he was backing off. It was as if he had decided to bide his time and, in so doing, give her time. If she stayed, she wondered how long this new approach would last.

If she stayed . . .

Of course, there was no question of her staying, but Robin found it unbearably difficult to decide on the moment she would actually leave.

Tuesday, all the new guests arrived to fill the vacant rooms of the inn, and the fresh country air left them all starving. No leftovers remained of the dinner Robin prepared that night.

Wednesday, Donal Caldwell surprised everyone by telling them he was checking out the next day. An art gallery in Los Angeles had arranged for a showing of his paintings, and he wanted to be there to help set it up to best advantage. Robin couldn't convince herself to leave without saying goodbye to Donal.

Thursday, Donal left. And on Thursday night, Robin knew she was making excuses. To force her hand, she packed her bags, readying them for the following evening. After a long debate with herself, she decided to leave a note but nothing else.

On her last night at Heron's Inn, Robin let her thoughts drift back over the weeks she had spent there, from her first hesitant moments as a stranger to this very evening, when she felt right at home. Even considering everything that had happened, she was glad she had come. She'd been of help to some of them.

There was a marked difference in David that she could claim some credit for, a difference in the way he and Eric related to each other. The relationship wasn't perfect, but there were signs that it could grow better. She had helped Barbara with her wedding. In a quick email sent from Hawaii, Barbara had thanked her again for the beautiful cakes. And with Eric . . .

Robin shied away from thinking too much about Eric.

Daylight came at a snail's pace. The sky was overcast, which caused the sun to put in a late appearance. All morning, time seemed to drag. Close to noon, the sun finally appeared to burn away the fog and take the grayness from the day. But the grayness of Robin's spirit could not be lifted. She pretended otherwise, but she knew she wasn't wholly convincing. Each time she spoke with someone, she wondered if that might be the last time she would see them.

The twins helped her make a batch of cookies. Almost as much cookie dough ended up in their stomachs as on the baking sheets, but Robin enjoyed their company. She smiled when each snitched a freshly baked treat and ran outside to play.

For what must have been the hundredth time, Robin checked her watch. This time, Samantha caught her.

"Are you waiting for a train or something?" she teased.

Robin tried to smile. "No . . . just thinking about dinner."

"You've been thinking about dinner a lot today. This isn't the first time I've seen you do that."

"Today just feels . . . odd, that's all."

"Don't tell me you have premonitions, too!"

"Who else does?"

"Bridget."

"I should have known."

"Bridget told me she likes you." Samantha paused. "You know, Robin, I really do appreciate having you here while Bridget's away. And not just because of Eric and David and everything. But because . . . I was really lonely when Bridget left. I didn't realize how often she and I sat around and talked. You could have been some kind of ogre and not been any fun to talk to at all. But you aren't. And I just want to say thanks."

Further evidence that in a small way she had been of help to another of the Marshalls. Robin's heart beat sorely. "Well, you're quite welcome," she said. She wanted to add, "Come talk to me anytime," but she couldn't. It would be another lie.

"Has Eric told you what I plan to do this fall?" Samantha asked brightly, not sensing Robin's inner turmoil.

The young woman continued to chatter, and Robin did her best to follow, but there wasn't much that sank in.

A short time later, David came into the kitchen. "Would you like some help with dinner?" he asked.

Robin smiled. "All offers are gratefully accepted."

"What are we making tonight?" he asked, stepping up to the sink to wash his hands.

Robin had thought to do something special, something that would really impress their palates, but in the end she decided it was best to finish as she'd begun. "I thought a nice roast, vegetables, homemade bread . . . that kind of thing."

"Better make a lot of it. This group certainly enjoys their food."

While he dried his hands, he grinned at her. He still wore his favorite clothes, but he had exchanged the swinging earring for a less flashy stud. His hair was contained by a rubber band. And, most important, the hostility had almost completely disappeared from his young face.

"What would you like me to do first?" he asked.

Robin couldn't help herself. She leaned across and gave him a quick, hard hug.

"What was that for?" he asked, laughing as she pulled back.

"It's a reward, because you're trying so hard."

He dismissed her compliment with a shrug. "I don't want any rewards."

She couldn't tell him, but at that moment he sounded so much like Eric.

She started to say something else, only to be interrupted when Allison rushed into the room with a worried frown.

"Have either of you seen the twins?" she asked.

"I did about an hour ago," Robin said. "They helped me make cookies."

"And not since? David, have you?"

David and Robin both answered in the negative.

Allison's frown deepened. "They were supposed to check in with me a half hour ago and they didn't."

"The last time I saw them, they went outside to play," Robin murmured.

"They probably lost track of time," David suggested.

"That little boy visiting down the street is completely uncontrolled," Allison complained. "His parents don't seem to care where he is or what he's doing."

"Have you looked outside yet?" David asked.

"Around the inn, yes."

"I saw them making sand forts on the beach yesterday," Robin said.

Allison's jaw tightened. "I told them not to do that again. Their clothes were coated with sand. It will probably take two or three washings to get it all out."

"They were having fun," David said.

"They can have fun in a cleaner way! I'm the one who has to clean up after them, David, not you."

"I'll try to remember that," David murmured.

Allison sent him an impatient look that was tinged with mounting worry. "This isn't exactly the safest place in the world. The cliffs, the water . . . but they love to come here."

"That's probably *why* they love to come here," David said wisely.

The contrariness of children's thought processes wasn't something Allison wanted to discuss at that moment. She released a sound between a hiss and a sigh and opened one of the French doors. "I'll check the beach," she said tensely before going outside.

David shook his head as she left but said nothing.

"It's better to worry too much than too little," Robin murmured.

"Something in between would be best."

Robin tilted her head and gave him a slow smile. "How did you get to be such an expert?"

"I spent years being a problem child."

Robin's smile widened. "Makes sense," she agreed, and they both started to laugh.

A full half-hour passed before Allison returned, red-faced and winded, her anxiety reaching yet another level. "They're not there!" she cried. "I looked all over and I didn't see them. I even checked the neighbor's house, thinking they might be there. But they're not!"

"Would you like some help to look for them?" Robin asked, abandoning her work.

"Yes! I don't know why, but I — I have a bad feeling about this."

"I'll get Eric and Samantha," David volun-

288

teered. He ran up the rear stairs.

The fear in Allison's eyes was hard to witness. Robin knew that it most likely sprang from Allison's experiences with her parents, from the fact that the two people she had loved most in the world had been taken from her without warning. She was afraid that it was going to happen again.

"I'm sure they're fine," Robin said, trying to console her. "They're most likely off exploring somewhere."

"They're not supposed to leave this part of Dunnigan Bay," Allison returned tightly.

Heavy footsteps sounded on the narrow stairs before Eric, David and Samantha filed into the room.

"David told us what's happened," Eric said. Then, unknowingly echoing Robin's words, he encouraged, "I'm sure they're fine. But it won't hurt to round them up. Let's start with the neighbors — all the neighbors."

"I'll check with Mrs. Wilson," David said, "and the houses on both sides of her."

"I'll take the others," Samantha said.

"Good. Then check the trails," Eric told them. "I'll take the cliff path. Robin . . . maybe you should stay here with Allison. I know —" He held up a hand when his sister started to protest. "But what if they come back and no one is here? If anyone finds them or they show up on their own, ring the bell, loud and long, okay? To let the rest of us know."

Robin had thought the old bell attached to the side of the house at the edge of the front porch to be purely decorative. Now it turned out to have a function.

Everyone nodded and those with outside assignments hurried away.

Allison couldn't sit still. With arms crossed tightly, she paced the floor.

"Would you like some tea or coffee?" Robin asked, thinking that a hot drink would help fortify the worried mother.

Allison shook her head. "If anything has happened to them . . ." she moaned. "It's been over an hour since they were supposed to report in."

The guests at the inn had scattered after breakfast that morning. Only the family and Robin remained. The old house was quiet. Too quiet.

Allison stood at the open front door, arms still crossed as if for reassurance, her gaze fastened upon the street. Suddenly she turned around. "I've just thought of something. Maybe they were digging a new fort and it collapsed! Digging tunnels in the sand is dangerous, isn't it? All that sand and dirt —"

"Wouldn't you have noticed?"

"I wasn't looking for anything like that! I thought — I was angry." She started to cry.

"We can settle that question very easily," Robin said, striving to keep Allison calm. "I'll go down and take a look. Then you can put your mind at rest in that area, at least."

Allison grasped her arm. "You'd do that?"

"Of course."

Allison looked away. "I haven't been very nice to you."

"Don't worry about it," Robin stated with finality.

"Thanks." Allison drew a shaky breath. "Yes, please. I'd like you to check."

Robin patted her hand and hurried out the door. Outside, she heard the wind-muffled calls of the twins' names. She broke into a run once she reached the street. Was it possible that her odd feeling about the day wasn't due entirely to her planned departure? That instead it portended something else? A danger to the children? That thought made her run even faster.

At the beach, she searched the sand and the grass line. She saw the remains of the fort the children had dug yesterday — long shallow ditches in the shape of a square.

Nothing like the kind of construction Allison was worried about. But that didn't mean the children couldn't have moved to a new location and begun a more complicated structure.

Robin moved beyond the grass line, eyes searching left and right. Then she heard a sound: a child's voice, carried on the wind. Her body stiffened, while her head turned in an age-old gesture of acute listening. She heard the sound again.

It came from over the water.

CHAPTER FIFTEEN

Robin darted to the water's edge, narrowing her eyes against the glare of the early afternoon sun. At first she didn't see anything, then slowly her gaze focused on a dark object bobbing awkwardly on the windswept waves more than halfway to the twin rock pillars. It was a boat, more precisely a small skiff. She could see an oar hover over the water, then jerk high into the air. Either the children didn't know how to row very well or they were in some kind of difficulty.

"Gwen!" she cried, cupping her hands around her mouth like a megaphone. "Colin!" A gust of wind whipped her words back over the sand. "Gwen!" she tried again.

A far-off voice answered. "Ro . . . bin!"

Robin glanced back toward the inn. She needed to alert everyone. Possibly Eric had access to another boat. She was afraid the children weren't going to make it back on their own.

"Gwen . . . Colin . . . don't do anything! Wait!" she yelled as loudly as she could. "I'll find someone to help you! Don't —" But before the last admonition had left her mouth, she saw the bow of the boat rise up and flip over. "Oh, no," she breathed, even as she heard the children's screams. "No!" she repeated.

Her heart pounded and her breathing was ragged. There was only one thing to do. She kicked off her shoes, slipped out of her jacket and ran into the water. She was barely aware of its coldness.

Once, long ago — in another life, it sometimes seemed — she hadn't been a very strong swimmer. Years of practice had changed that, years of determination that never again would she put another person's life at risk in order to save her from drowning.

When the water reached her hips, she dived forward. Now the cold hit her like a knife, jerking the air from her lungs. She pressed forward, jeans sticking to her legs, wishing that her blouse was thicker.

She treaded water for a moment to get a better bearing on the children, to be sure that, if they could, they had stayed with the overturned boat. Three heads bobbed in the water, only two of them close by the vessel. The other person was a distance away, too far to grab hold. Robin wasn't sure how long they could stay afloat, especially the one who was farther from the boat. From past experience, Robin knew that coldness and fright quickly robbed a person of strength, particularly a child.

Just as she redoubled her effort, she heard the inn's bell start to clang. Someone else must have seen what had happened and been in a position to alert the others.

Eric had trotted along the trail as far as the branch leading to the beach. He'd yelled the children's names repeatedly. If they were there, they would have heard him, on the beach or somewhere off the cliff trail away from the water. He was sure of that. It was possible they'd gone to the Overlook, but he doubted they would disobey their mother that purposefully. He retraced his steps, continuing periodically to yell. Then he heard the bell.

Someone had found them! They were safe. But the sound of the bell grew more frantic. Something was wrong. He covered the ground like the athlete he once had been in school, only to stop where the cliff's edge started to curve down along the trail to

Dunnigan Bay. One sweeping glance told him the story. Three children in the water, more than half the distance to the mouth of the bay, and one person — Robin, from the color of her hair — swimming out to help them.

People were hurrying down the street — family, neighbors, friends. But he was closest if he went straight down. Robin couldn't possibly do it all on her own. The children who were clinging to the boat might not be able to hold on long enough for her to make two more trips.

As the cliff curved into Dunnigan Bay, it lost some of its height and steepness. Eric leapt over the edge, digging his heels into the loose dirt and rock, jumping from spot to spot, somehow keeping his balance as he descended the thirty or so feet to the water. At the bay's edge, he peeled off his thick sweater and his heavy shoes, then made a shallow dive into the cold water.

He came up, took a deep breath and began a battle against the wind-whipped waves. On most days, the bay was fairly calm. Today, it churned. He fought on and on, not thinking of anything but the struggling children and Robin. Then it dawned on him: this must have been the way his father felt when he had gone in after the girl. It didn't matter how she had gotten into trouble, just that she had. And he had been there to help her.

Eric pushed the revelation into a back corner of his mind. That would be something to contemplate later. Right now, he couldn't think of it.

He had to act.

Robin became aware of Eric's presence as she neared the first child. She saw his strong strokes make steady headway across the water, and she could have cried aloud in relief. She hadn't been sure how she would handle the situation. She doubted that she could right the boat, and she also doubted that the children's strength would allow them to wait in the cold while she went back for help, since hypothermia became more and more of a danger as time wore on.

"Robin!" Gwen cried hoarsely, gagging as a rising crest hit her face. Though the girl did the best she could to stay afloat, her situation was clearly growing desperate.

In several strokes Robin was beside her, supporting her with her free arm. "Are you hurt?" she asked quickly.

Gwen shook her head, her teeth chattering. "Colin and Teddy," she said, straining to see the other children.

"They're going to be fine," Robin assured her. "Your Uncle Eric is coming for them."

Gwen started to cry.

"Hey, it's all right." Robin tried to sound reassuring. "The worst part is over."

"I didn't want to come in the first place," Gwen wailed. "Colin and Teddy made me!"

"We'll talk about that later, okay? Right now, grab hold of my shoulders." She shifted so that her back was to Gwen. "No, higher," she said as Gwen reached for her upper arms. "That's right," she approved when finally the girl found the appropriate position.

Eric arrived at the capsized boat. "Are you all right?" he called to her.

"Fine! We're going in. Is everything going to be all right with you three?"

"I'll hoist them onto the bottom of the boat," he said. "We'll be right behind you."

"Do you need help?"

"No."

Robin spoke again to Gwen. "Relax, let me do all the work. You just hold on. Are you ready?"

Teeth still chattering, Gwen nodded.

Robin began to swim a modified breaststroke, letting the wind and the waves help her progress this time instead of hindering her. She glanced at Eric. He was doing

298

exactly as he'd said. One boy was already out of the water, straddling the keel, the other was being given a boost. Eric waved to her, then moved to the front of the boat and started to tow it by executing a powerful sidestroke.

It seemed to take a long time to reach the shore, but Robin knew that time only felt drawn out. Her muscles were starting to burn, since Gwen's hold had shifted to her neck. Trying not to think too much, she pushed on.

She waved David away when he paused while swimming out to help Eric with the boat. She and Gwen were all right. They were going to make it.

The small crowd on the beach surged forward as the swimmers reached shallow water. Allison splashed into the surf, unmindful of her cream linen slacks. She drew Gwen into her arms, all the while crying and saying her daughter's name over and over.

It was only then that Robin realized the full import of what she'd done. She had saved Martin Marshall's granddaughter from the same fate as the one he'd saved her from. That thought, along with the physical strain she'd just been through, made her knees buckle as she tried to stand.

Samantha rushed over with a blanket, and someone helped her back to her feet. Pats on the back greeted her, some given by people she couldn't remember ever meeting before. She sank onto the sand again, this time protected from the wind and the waves.

Attention switched to the new arrivals, and the crowd once again surged forward. Robin saw a flash of boat and the two children being plucked from its keel. Allison was hugging both her son and her daughter, while Teddy's parents greeted him with shock and relief. David stood to one side of the group, a blanket wrapped around his shoulders.

Robin struggled to her feet. Everyone was accounted for except Eric. On legs that felt like limp spaghetti, she made her way toward the crowd. People parted, letting her through. Then she saw what they were all looking at. At the edge of the surf, a man's body lay sprawled on his back on the sand, arms and legs lax, while someone — Samantha? — bent over him.

Even though she couldn't see his upper body or face, Robin knew it was Eric. She jerked forward, fear clutching her heart. *Eric!* she cried in her mind. "Eric!" she breathed aloud, not wanting to believe the conclusion her intellect had jumped to. It couldn't be . . . it just couldn't be. Fate wouldn't be that unkind.

She scrambled across the last few feet on her hands and knees, no longer able to walk. The person blocking her view pulled away. Then Robin saw him at last.

It was Eric, but it wasn't Eric. A roaring started in Robin's ears, a sound that increased until all other sound was obliterated.

"Robin?" she heard someone say from far off, as if they were speaking into a deep chamber.

Her attention was riveted on the man lying on the sand. Martin Marshall . . . Eric. Eric . . . Martin Marshall. He looked so much like his father, even under normal circumstances. And now, as he lay there wet, drowned, wearing the same tiny gold medal, the two men melded into one person. It was as if all the years of Robin's life in between didn't exist.

She gave a heartrending cry and jumped onto the sand next to him. Then she started pounding on his chest, shaking him, trying to force him back to life. She couldn't live through it again. If he didn't live, she wouldn't live.

"No!" she screamed in wild determination. *"No!"*

Hands grasped her arms, pushing her back. Blinded by her tears, she fought the person who tried to interfere.

"Robin!" a voice commanded sternly.

"No! I have to . . . it can't happen again! It can't! I can't let it!"

"Robin!"

Slowly, something in the timbre of the voice penetrated Robin's hysteria.

"Robin, listen to me," Eric said. He was sitting up. "I'm all right. I'm not hurt. I'm not drowned."

Robin's heart raced, her lungs couldn't get enough air.

Samantha leaned across Eric to smooth her wet hair. "You really freaked out, Robin," she said shakily.

"She thought I was dead," Eric said.

Robin couldn't pull herself back to the present. She stared at him blankly. Sixteen years was a long time to travel back and forth in a panic. Her gaze dropped to the medal. It wasn't her imagination. She recognized it now . . . from then. Her gaze returned to his.

Water dripped from his hair to roll down the sides of his face. Someone had placed a blanket across his shoulders and settled hers back into place.

Their gazes never deviated from each

other. Then Robin was aware of something shifting in Eric's mind, a question posed and suddenly answered as he made the fateful connection.

"Who *are* you?" Eric whispered intently. But it was apparent he already knew.

Sensing that something had gone horribly wrong but not knowing what, Samantha tried to placate him. "She's Robin, Eric."

"No, she's not," he returned. His voice sounded oddly hollow.

Samantha shook her head, making her loose blond curls dance in the wind. "You're going into shock," she decided, determined to find a simple explanation. "We need to get you all inside. Allison! We need to take them to the inn."

Eric stood up. He made no attempt to help Robin. Instead, David hurried over to steady her on her feet.

Robin tried to ignore the curious looks as she passed through the dwindling crowd. Gwen and Colin were rushed ahead, while she and the others followed. Teddy and his relatives had already left for their house, where dry warm clothes — and most probably a stern lecture — awaited.

If only she could feel something, Robin thought. But she seemed drained of all emotion. He knew! Yet all she could do was keep walking, step by step, like a zombie moving among the living.

She was rushed upstairs, forced into a warm tub, toweled off, wrapped in Samantha's oversize white terry robe and brought to the family room, where a hot cup of tea awaited her. The twins were already there, smelling of soap and wrapped in fresh blankets, mugs of hot chocolate in their hands.

"We wanted to see the sea lions up close," Colin said meekly in defense of their escapade. "They were playing by the rock towers and we thought . . . it didn't look all that far!"

"Teddy found the boat," Gwen added.

David came into the room, dressed warmly in dry jeans and a dark sweater. He settled on the couch next to the twins.

"You shouldn't have even thought about it without asking for permission," Allison said sternly. "It was a silly thing to do. If Robin and your Uncle Eric hadn't seen you . . ." She took a deep breath. "And you should thank your Uncle David, too. He didn't have to do what he did."

"Thank you, Uncle David," the children said together. "Thank you, Robin."

"And don't forget Uncle Eric when he comes in."

"We won't," Gwen promised, squirming.

Robin felt the adults' curious glances, yet she couldn't react. Did a condemned prisoner sometimes feel the same way just before the ax fell or the rope jerked? Nothing? No pain, no fear — only a great, gaping emptiness?

Eric entered the room, and the level of tension immediately heightened. He carried anger with him the way others might carry joy. He walked to the bookcase where the photo albums were kept and withdrew a slim volume from one of the shelves. When he opened it, several newspaper clippings fluttered to the floor. He bent to retrieve only one. As he straightened, his eyes moved from it to Robin.

"One of you take the twins downstairs," he said quietly, but with such authority that no one questioned him. The twins jumped up and Allison followed.

David stayed where he was on the couch and Samantha perched uneasily on the upholstered arm. Robin was alone where she sat farther away.

Eric stood in front of her and extended the yellowed clipping. "This is who you really are, isn't it?"

Robin's eyes slid away from the image of her own twelve-year-old face. It was a picture that had been taken while she was leaving the beach shortly after Martin Marshall had died. In one corner, a section of the ambulance was visible.

Eric handed the clipping to David, who passed it on to Samantha. Robin saw their startled exchange of looks.

"Isn't it?" Eric insisted.

Robin lifted her gaze to him. He, too, had showered and changed into jeans and a patterned shirt, which he hadn't bothered to tuck in. "Yes," she admitted huskily.

"Get out," he ordered coldly, with no hesitation.

"Eric!" Samantha cried, jumping to her feet. "You can't do that! Even if she is — even if she . . ." She ran out of steam.

"I said get out, and I meant it," Eric repeated.

Still, Robin could feel no pain. She stumbled to her feet and started to walk away.

"Eric! You can't — you have to stop her!" Samantha cried. "There must be a reason! Maybe she didn't know. Maybe — Robin? Robin, say something!"

David remained very still, very quiet. He refused to meet her gaze. She looked at Eric. Cold, hard contempt streamed steadily from his eyes and she understood why all emotion within her had been temporarily blanked out. The onrush of pain would have been too great.

As it was, no sound would pass her lips. All she could do was stand there, pleading mutely for understanding.

Her plea fell on dry soil as far as Eric was concerned. "Call her by her real name," he said harshly. "Roberta . . . Roberta Farrell."

The hated name. The hated person. Robin turned away. This time, no one tried to stop her.

Robin got as far as her bedroom before she started to cry. Huge tears rolled down over her cheeks as she covered her mouth with both hands. The worst had happened. She'd been found out. One more day! All she'd needed was one more day, and then she would have been gone. No one would have had to know. They could remember her with warm thoughts, not bitter ones.

She sat down on the edge of the mattress and collapsed onto her side, sobs continuing to rack her body. He hated her. They all hated her. They felt betrayed. And there was absolutely nothing she could say or do that would make them feel differently. She had no defense. She'd known from the first exactly what she was doing. She'd even planned it, going so far as to invent her references. But she hadn't meant to hurt them. She'd never meant to cause them any harm.

She had fit in so well here, because she was just as much a part of them as they were of her. And now that she had come to care for them — to love Eric — knowing that she'd caused them additional pain was torture to her. It was a punishment she would carry with her for the rest of her life. Not content to leave well enough alone, she'd made a bad situation worse. Good intentions didn't count, not in the real world.

She sat up and rubbed at her cheeks, trying to erase all evidence of her tears. He wanted her to leave, just as she always had known that he would if ever he learned the truth. Her bags were packed. She could be out of the house in five minutes. She went to the wardrobe and dragged the suitcases outside.

Someone knocked at her door. Robin's heart leapt. Eric! Then reality asserted itself. If Eric was at the door, it would be to castigate her for taking too long.

"Who is it?" she called softly.

"Samantha. Please, let me in."

Robin opened the door a crack. She had a

hard time meeting the young woman's eyes. "Tell Eric I'm on my way. I won't be five minutes."

"I want to talk to you, Robin. Please, let me in."

Robin braced herself for more anger as she opened the door. Samantha came in, followed by Allison. At the sight of the older sister, Robin's stomach tightened. Allison had been suspicious of her from the first time they'd met. She had warned her not to hurt Eric. Robin didn't think she could stand it if Allison started to attack her again.

Samantha sat on the edge of the bed and looked at the suitcases. "I saw them earlier," she said. "When I came looking for something for you to wear. That's why I loaned you my robe."

Robin glanced down at what she was wearing. With everything she'd been through, she hadn't paid any attention to the robe. "I'll leave it on the bed," she said tightly. Her gaze moved to Allison. *Get it over with,* she thought edgily.

Allison surprised her by giving a strained smile. "Samantha told me," she said. "I don't understand, but after what you did for Gwen and Colin, I can't be totally against you."

"Robin," Samantha cut in, then corrected

herself. "Roberta. Why didn't you tell us? Why did you keep it a secret?" It was more of a plea than a demand.

"What could I say?" Robin asked.

"I thought we were friends."

"We were."

"Then?"

"Would we ever have become friends if I had told you the truth in the beginning? I doubt it. Eric —"

"I love Eric dearly, you know that," Samantha interrupted. "But I don't let him tell me what to think or who to have for a friend."

"This is different," Robin said stiffly.

Allison watched her steadily. "What are you going to do? Where are you going to go? Do you have a place?"

"Yes," Robin answered through a tightening throat.

"We don't blame you for what happened in the past, Roberta," Samantha said. "I thought you understood that. Eric might blame you, but we don't."

"My name is Robin," Robin murmured. "It's a nickname."

Samantha smiled thinly. "See? You didn't lie about everything."

Robin turned away.

"You and your big mouth," Allison

grumbled with sisterly directness. "Here, take this," she said, holding out a small card to Robin. "It has my address and phone number in Palo Alto. If you ever need anything, don't hesitate to call. And I mean that. You helped save my children's lives."

After Robin took the card, Allison stepped into the hall, closing the door behind her.

Robin released a trembling sigh. Samantha hugged her. "Maybe Eric will change his mind," she said. "I know he loves you. Right now, he's just . . . hurt."

"It's more than that and you know it. If I had it to do over again, I wouldn't come here. I'm as bad as the twins. I should have thought things through. David, too. I hope he doesn't . . ."

Robin couldn't finish, but Samantha understood. "He's made so much progress."

"I was going to leave tonight," Robin whispered.

"I thought that."

"I should have left yesterday. Then everything . . ."

Samantha smiled wryly. "Things have a way of *not* working out. But who knows? Maybe this time they will. They did for the twins."

"Take care of Eric . . . and David . . . and tell Barbara and Benjamin . . ." Robin bit her trembling lip. They were as close to brothers and sisters as she would ever have. And now she'd lost them.

"I will," Samantha promised. "I'll be in San Francisco in the fall. Do you think you'll be there then?"

"I don't know," Robin said honestly. "I don't have any idea." She might go back to New York or to Europe. She wasn't sure if she'd be able to stay on the West Coast. Every time she looked at the Pacific, the memories would overwhelm her.

Minutes later, Robin slid her suitcases into the trunk of her car and closed the lid. As she settled behind the wheel, she saw David standing at the edge of the kitchen garden. He hesitated, as if of two minds whether to approach her. Finally he made a decision.

Unshed tears blurred Robin's eyes as she watched him come nearer — tall, very thin, very young, very dear. She brushed the moisture from her lashes.

He stopped at the driver's door and bent to look at her. "So, you're just going to leave," he said curtly.

"I'm doing what Eric said to do."

"And not even say goodbye," he continued as if she hadn't spoken.

"I didn't think you'd want me to."

312

David kicked the dirt. "That was a pretty lousy thing to do!"

"Not saying goodbye?" Robin asked facetiously.

Her pathetic attempt to lighten the atmosphere between them failed miserably. His pale blue eyes speared her as he corrected, "Not telling us who you are. What else did you forget to mention? You did a pretty good job on me. Are you a shrink or something?"

"A psychiatrist? Me?" she responded, genuinely surprised.

He narrowed his eyes, measuring the truth of her words. "I guess not," he murmured after a moment.

"David, I didn't mean to hurt anyone, especially you. I thought — I thought, if I came here —"

"Was it all some kind of joke to you? To see how gullible we are?"

"No!"

"To get us to trust you? To get us to tell you things?"

"No! David, I —"

"To get us to love you?"

Robin closed her eyes, because they'd suddenly become flooded with tears again. Moisture slipped from the edges. She shook her head. "I didn't mean for any of this to happen! All I wanted was to meet you all, to see if there was anything I could do to help."

David laughed shortly. "And you found plenty of room for that, didn't you?" He stepped back. "Oh, go on! Go back to wherever it is you come from. Go back to pretending that we don't exist."

"David, please. Listen to me for a minute. It wasn't like that. *I'm* not like that." She took a bracing breath. "Don't . . . don't give up on yourself again. You have so much to contribute. A good mind. A fine spirit. If you want to be a chef, be one! Don't let anyone stop you. Not even me."

He shook his head, saying quietly, "Somehow that just doesn't play the same anymore." Then he gave her a long last look and turned back toward the garden.

Robin watched him move away with a feeling of powerlessness. There were so many things she wanted to say. But would he value any of them? She had abused his trust.

"David!" she tried again, but he kept walking.

Her grip on the steering wheel was like a lifeline. She didn't want to leave them like this. But she had lost all power, all influence. Like a disgraced member of an ancient tribal society, she was being cast out.

CHAPTER SIXTEEN

Eric heard the car start and moments later pull away. But he didn't look. He wouldn't allow himself, because he might try to stop her.

"One of us will have to make dinner tonight," he said to the room at large. Samantha and Allison sat silently on the camel-colored couch. "Tomorrow I'll place another ad. It shouldn't be too long before someone suitable answers."

"You were wrong to send her away, Eric," Allison said.

"I was left with no other choice."

"She was going to leave tonight anyway," Samantha said, surprising both him and Allison.

"How do you know that?" Allison asked.

"She told me."

Eric laughed hollowly. "And you believed her?"

"I believed her. Also, she had her cases

packed. A person doesn't do that without planning to use them."

After a moment spent digesting this information, Eric asked, "Is that supposed to make a difference?"

"It should tell you that she didn't mean for this to happen," Samantha said in her defense.

"Or that she thought she was about to get caught!" Eric contradicted brusquely.

"How can you say that?" Samantha demanded.

"It's easy," he answered.

From the corner of his eye, Eric saw Allison touch Samantha's arm and give a tiny shake of her head. He turned on her. "And don't try to tell me I didn't have good reason! She lied to us, to all of us!"

"I still feel your actions were extreme," Allison retorted. "Look what she'd just done for Gwen and Colin."

"Look what she did for us all those years ago," Eric countered.

"We can't change the past, Eric," Samantha broke in.

He jerked to his feet. "I'm not going to listen to this. I did what I felt was right."

"But if you love her . . ."

Samantha's unfinished sentence rang in Eric's ears as he walked to his room and slammed the door. To hear his sisters talk, he was the one in the wrong. Not her. Not Robin . . . Roberta . . . *Robin.* He couldn't call her anything else.

He started to pace. She'd played him for a fool from the very beginning. Then slowly, insidiously, she'd wormed her way into his family, uncaring of how they would feel when the truth eventually came out. And it had to come out. Did she plan some kind of grand denouement? An announcement, with all of them in attendance? Did she think that just because she'd suckered them into accepting her, into loving her, that it could make up for the past?

He sat down at his desk and dragged over a stack of paperwork. At the end of an hour, he'd reduced the stack considerably. But he had done nothing to reduce the pain in his heart.

Eric tried to go on. He tried to forget her. But she had become too much a part of their existence. Everywhere he looked there were reminders of her.

After Allison and the twins went back to Palo Alto at the end of their holiday, he interviewed four people for the job of cook. Three were awful, one he hired. A man this time, who had experience as a short-order cook. Eric checked his references with meticulous care.

Barbara and Timothy came back from their honeymoon and were shocked to hear of Robin's duplicity. Of course, Barbara sided with her sisters. *He* was the one in the wrong.

Benjamin heard the story out, uttered a contemplative "Hmm" and said he'd try to be up the next weekend, only he didn't make it.

David reacted in characteristic fashion, by keeping his thoughts and emotions to himself. But in David, Eric knew that he had an ally. The boy had been hurt. *He* didn't try to make excuses for her behavior.

Possibly because of their mutual feeling of betrayal, relations between himself and David continued to improve, though there was still a lot of circling and wariness.

At the three-week point, late one night, David sought him out. Eric sat at his desk, again doing paperwork — work that had never before received quite so much dedication. David hitched a seat a short distance from Eric's elbow and said, "I've been thinking about something."

Eric leaned back and looked at him. "What?"

"I want to learn to be a chef."

Strong memories of Robin stormed across Eric's senses. His stomach tightened. "Why?" he asked simply, bracing himself for the answer. Robin's name hadn't been spoken in a number of days.

"Because . . . I enjoy working with food. I think I could be good at it."

Eric shifted position in his chair. "Is that enough of a reason?" he asked.

David hesitated, then he said, "Robin says it is."

"You've been talking to her?" Eric asked tautly.

"When she was here. Not since. And before she left, she told me I should do it, if that was what I wanted. And I think it is."

Eric frowned. "How can you give credence to anything she said?"

"That's what I've been thinking about." A newfound maturity had started to build in his youngest brother's eyes. A new seriousness. "I think maybe we've been wrong about her."

Eric could stand it no more. He lurched from his chair, shaking his head. "Not you, too! She lied to us, David. *Lied* to us. She knew how we felt."

"She knew how *you* felt."

"Why did she give us a false name? Why did she pretend that she didn't know anything about us, when she knew almost as much as we know ourselves?"

"That's one of the things that's been bothering me," David said. "What did she have to gain? I can't see anything."

"To satisfy her morbid curiosity, that's what! Some people are like that, Davey. They like to go to terrible house fires. They like to watch horrible wrecks. That's the way she is."

David shook his head. "No, I don't believe that."

"She's been a curse on this family from the very beginning."

"That's another thing," David said, undeterred. "You told me before that it's not possible for a two-year-old to be responsible for someone's death. If either you or I or Robin had died trying to rescue the twins, would they be responsible? They're ten years old, just a little younger than Robin was when Dad died rescuing her. They were where they shouldn't have been, doing something they shouldn't have been doing. How is that different from her?"

"It's different, okay?"

"You're being unreasonable, and that's not like you, Eric."

"How do you know what's 'like me'?" Eric demanded, striking out in his lonely pain.

"Up to now, you haven't cared very much."

"Robin helped me to see that I was wrong."

"Robin! Robin!" Eric shouted in frustration.

David stood up. "If I were you, I'd do some hard thinking. If I loved someone as much as you obviously love her, I hope I'd be able to get past my own bullheadedness and tell her that I do."

"I'm not bullheaded."

David smiled slowly. "You're the king of bullheaded. Go find her. Talk to her. See what *she* has to say. So far, you're the one who's done all the talking."

Eric's fists worked at his sides. "You're still pretty insolent, aren't you, kid?" he said tightly. Then he released all the tension that had built up in his body. "And you've also turned out to be pretty smart."

"You'll take my advice?"

"Maybe," Eric replied noncommittally. But they both knew that he would.

As David passed by him on his way to the door, he tapped him on the shoulder for good luck.

Robin fitted the key into the lock of her apartment door. But before she could turn it, she was aware of someone moving toward her from beside the tall leafy plant that decorated the landing. Her first instinct was to cry out. Her next reaction, upon recognition of the person, was relief, which instantly turned to alarm. Eric!

She turned to guard her door, as if he were an unwelcome intruder. "What do you want? How did you find me?" she charged. She couldn't let him see how shattered she felt.

"May I come in?" he asked quietly.

"I'd rather you didn't," she replied.

He looked so dear to her, so true to the picture in her mind's eye — the hair, the eyes, the way he smiled. He smiled ever so slightly now.

"I suppose we could conduct our business out here on the landing, but it is rather late."

"Why are you here?" she asked again.

"I want to talk to you."

"I thought you'd already said all you have to say."

"Obviously not. Otherwise, why would I be here?"

"Maybe I don't want to listen."

"Is that the truth?"

"Would you believe me if I said it was?"

"That's what I'd like to talk to you about."

Robin gave her head a short, angry shake. But she wasn't really angry. It was just a surface emotion to cover all the other, more complex emotions that took turns surging through her.

"I'll give you ten minutes," she said. Then with steady fingers that belied her inner turmoil, she turned the key in the lock and swept open the door.

Never in Robin's wildest dreams since her dejected return had she expected to see Eric Marshall inside her apartment. He made no attempt to hide his curiosity as she clicked on a switch and a subtle lighting system sprang to life. He looked around at the furnishings, at the evidence of her sophisticated taste. "Very nice," he murmured.

"The clock is ticking," she reminded him.

"A little more than a part-time student, part-time cook can afford."

She tapped a foot. She'd gone back to her old job at Le Jardin after learning that Marla and Jean-Pierre had yet to hire a replacement. With the resumption of her work there, she'd returned to her accustomed schedule of going in at two or three in the afternoon and coming home close to midnight. Yet her heart wasn't in it. It wasn't the same.

His smile broadened, then he took a seat on her couch and patted the cushion at his side.

She crossed her arms, pointedly waiting.

"I found you," he said, "after I talked with Benjamin. He gave me the name of the restaurant you told him, as well as the name of the owner. And the owner — Simon — gave me your address."

"He wouldn't do that! Not so easily."

"Did I say it was easy?"

Robin wondered what he had told Simon. "You shouldn't have done that. He might worry."

"An old boyfriend of yours?" he asked.

"No. A friend, that's all."

Eric made no comment.

"That's still not telling me what you want," she stated.

"You," he said very quietly. She could easily have missed it.

Her knees wobbled. "Stop playing games with me," she demanded.

He sat forward. "This is about as far from a game as I can get. I was wrong when I told you to leave."

"Have you had a hard time finding someone else to cook for you?"

"No, a very competent man named Henry is filling in for us now."

He'd replaced her so easily! "Then why —"

"I was wrong," he said firmly, "when I

blamed you for causing our father's death."

Robin sat down in the chair closest to her, looking blankly at Eric. He reached for her hand and she didn't pull it away, because, at the moment, she was utterly incapable of doing so.

"I thought about it — David's advice, by the way — and I decided that all those years I blamed you, it wasn't your fault. You were a child. You were no more to blame than Gwen and Colin."

It sounded good, but how deeply did the newfound feeling run? Robin withdrew her hand, clutching it to the other.

"People tried to tell me that before," he continued, "but I wasn't prepared to listen. I could only see my point of view. But when I dived into the water after Colin and Teddy, I realized I'd been wrong to be angry with my father, too. Yes, he had family responsibilities. But he also had a responsibility to the girl — to you. He acted instinctively, just as I did. Just as you did. I doubt if he gave more than a passing thought to us. He saw that you were in danger, and he acted."

"You hate me for what happened," Robin whispered.

"Not anymore!"

She shook her head, rejecting what he said. "It goes too deep, Eric. It's like prejudice. That kind of feeling doesn't change overnight."

"It's been a lot of nights," he said softly.

Robin continued to shake her head. He slipped off the couch to kneel before her, covering her hands with both of his. "Robin," he said huskily, "I love you. Finding out who you are . . . has been difficult. But it doesn't make any difference to me now. I don't care if you were playing where you shouldn't have been —"

She stood up abruptly, breaking contact. "But I *wasn't* where I shouldn't have been. I was on the beach . . . walking! Looking for shells! Looking for sand dollars! I didn't do anything wrong!"

"Then you're all the less to blame!"

"No!" She drew a trembling breath. "This isn't going to work, Eric. This is exactly what I faced when I lived at Heron's Inn. If I told you who I was, you'd hate me. If I didn't tell you who I was, you'd hate me when you found out. It's true! I do love you. I love you more than — no! Don't touch me." She skittered away from his reach.

Eric used the chair to push himself to his feet. "I don't understand. If I love you, if you love me . . ."

"The past is what's the matter, Eric."

"Damn the past!"

327

"It's not that simple."

He ran a hand through his hair in frustration. "So what are we going to do? Give up? Live apart forever?"

Tears trembled on her lashes. "I don't know. I just know that at this moment, it isn't right. The past is too . . . close."

"This is crazy!"

"Your ten minutes are up."

He looked at her as if she'd hit him. "You can't expect me to leave with everything so unsettled."

"I'm asking you to leave. Please."

"When can I see you again?" he murmured tautly.

"I don't know."

"May I call you?"

"No."

His lips were tight, his body stiff as he moved to the front door. He opened it, turned to look at her, then he was gone.

Robin stayed very still. She didn't move until a siren sounded in the distance. Then she went to the computer and inserted the CD.

She settled in the chair and clicked the appropriate buttons. There she was, on the beach, in shock, afraid. There he was, Martin Marshall, unchanged over the years. When the video switched to the Marshall children, this time Robin was prepared. She muted the sound.

She didn't hear Benjamin cry.

The call came on a Sunday. From David. Robin greeted him warmly. She was glad that he wanted to make contact.

"It didn't surprise me when Eric said you were a professional chef," the boy said. "Or that you work at some fancy restaurant. You gave yourself away a couple of times. Remember?"

"I worked very hard to keep my secret."

"Why?" he asked directly.

"Because if I'd cooked for you the way I'm trained to cook, you would have known instantly that I was more than I claimed to be."

"I meant, why did you have to keep who you are such a secret? You could have told me. I wouldn't have told Eric."

"I was afraid."

"We wouldn't have eaten you . . . well, Eric might have." He cleared his throat. "I have something else I want to ask you, and something I want to tell. Which do you want first?"

"The question."

"All right. Which culinary academy do you recommend?"

"You've decided to go back to school?" she asked.

"Just tell me which one and I'll enroll. I've passed my French test, so I have the credit I need. I'll get my diploma."

"I'll ask the school to send you a brochure."

David said, "All right. Now, to the 'tell' part. Eric is eating himself alive up here. I've never seen him like this before. He barely talks, he barely eats. Samantha can't get through to him. I can't, either. He deals with the guests, but the rest of the time he just sits and stares."

Eric's behavior sounded very similar to her own. She cradled the telephone closer to her ear. "Has he said anything about me?" she ventured.

"Only that he saw you. I had to drag your telephone number out of him. If I didn't have to talk to you about the academy, I don't think he'd have given it to me."

Robin stared out the window over the bay. The city of San Francisco looked like a postcard across the water. The sun was shining, the air crisp and clear. But she longed for somewhere farther north. For a much different view.

David spoke again. "Samantha said to tell you that Eric's been punished enough."

330

Robin was startled. "I'm not punishing him!"

"That's what she said to tell you. I'm just passing it on."

"Tell Samantha . . . tell her I'll keep it in mind."

"Okay. You won't forget the brochure?"

"I'll call them as soon as I hang up."

"Aw-*rright!*" David crowed.

Robin hung up and looked at the calendar sitting on the table by the phone. Fifteen days had passed since she'd seen Eric. Fifteen bleak, torturous days.

She called up the academy in San Francisco and gave them David's address. Then she made another call to Marla at Le Jardin.

As soon as she got off the phone, she hurried to her bedroom and tossed a suitcase onto the bed, opening it as she also opened a drawer. Marla had been worried about her, just as David and Samantha had been worried about Eric. And, wonderful friend that she was, she'd immediately agreed to Robin's request.

With barely a thought to the thickening evening traffic, Robin rushed to her car and backed quickly out of her parking slot.

Dunnigan Bay was cloaked in a light fog

331

when Robin drove down its single street. The moon, struggling to shed light onto the earth below, lent the night a lustrous glow.

The lights at Heron's Inn were off, and a sleepy quietness pervaded the entire cove. Robin parked the car and walked quietly up the drive, pausing only long enough in the garden to see if anyone was there. No one was.

She tried one of the French doors. If it was locked, she would wait till morning. If not, she would slip inside. The door swung open to her touch.

She slipped into the room that she knew so well, the night-light from the hall providing enough illumination for her to see that the kitchen was still the same. Henry had done nothing to change it.

She made her way up the servants' stairway. Had Henry been given the use of Bridget's room, as well? Was he sleeping in her bed? Did he hang his clothing in the cleared section of her great old wardrobe? Robin felt a twinge of possessiveness, undoubtedly similar to what Bridget must have felt when she'd first heard of her own arrival.

She stepped into the hall on the third floor and turned toward the door where a weak light escaped through the bottom crack. In a strange way, she felt as if she'd never left Heron's Inn. Her heart rate increased as she stopped at the door and raised her curled hand. She paused, swallowed and gave a light rap with her knuckles.

Long seconds passed before Eric called out, "Just a minute."

He came to the door in bare feet, wearing only his jeans. When he saw her, his eyes widened in shocked surprise. "Robin?" he said blankly.

Neither shock nor surprise lasted very long. Both emotions were quickly replaced by exhilaration.

"Robin?" he said again as he pulled her into the room and into his arms.

He felt so wonderful, his body so warm and familiar, his kiss the promise of more to come.

Pulling back, he said, "How did you — how long — it's what . . . 2:00 a.m.?"

Robin slid away from him, holding herself in check. "It's late," she said softly.

"I don't really care what time it is — just that you're here."

He came toward her again, ready to wrap her in his arms, but she held him off by placing a hand on his chest.

"We still have to talk," she said.

"Now?"

"Now." She kept her hand firmly in place until he backed away a step.

She glanced around the room, the disarray provided evidence of the hours the room's occupant spent there. A newspaper was spread open on the desk, and an untouched cup of black coffee had grown cold. Several paperback mysteries were scattered, propped open, on the floor near the head of the bed. A shirt hung limply from an oak foot post.

"I wasn't expecting company," he murmured.

"Would you like me to leave?" she asked.

"No." His answer was quick.

"There are several things you have to understand," Robin began. She had had hours in which to rehearse what she would say. "When I first came here, I didn't have a plan. My only thought was to meet you, to get to know you . . . all of you. I'd known *about* you for years. You're not the only one to have newspaper clippings." She drew a breath. "I thought about all of you all the time. I couldn't get your family out of my mind. I wanted to meet you when I was a child, but my parents wouldn't let me. So later, when the time was right, I found a way. Only the more I got to know you, the more trapped I became, because of the way

I'd come to feel. I couldn't tell you who I was. You hated me."

"I don't hate you now."

"I know that. But this still has to be said." He took a short breath and waited.

She collected her thoughts. "I lied about who I was, because if I'd told you the truth, you wouldn't have hired me. So I made up a new identity. I became Robin McGrath. You don't know how many times I wished I *was* Robin McGrath. Robin McGrath wouldn't have had to watch every word she said or pretend she didn't know anything about your family's history. She could have loved you like you wanted to be loved, without regret, without the past getting in the way." She paused. "It wasn't easy, Eric."

"*I* didn't make it easy."

"There's something else," Robin said. "Something I think I owe you. I want to tell you about your dad. If he hadn't come in after me, Eric, I would have drowned for sure. There's no question that he saved my life. That one wave was so unexpected. One second I was on the beach, the next I was caught up in this huge surge of water, being dragged offshore." Her voice wavered. "Your dad . . . I don't know where he came from. I didn't see him until he'd grabbed hold of me. I was so afraid. I'd swallowed a lot of water. And I was so cold. Your dad was a strong swimmer. I tried to help, but we were pushed back and forth. We were thrown against the rocks, only he never let me hit them. I felt the impact through his body. We both went under several times." She started to cry silently, tears rolling down her cheeks. "He smiled at me. He told me to relax, that he wouldn't let anything bad happen to me. That was the last thing . . ."

Eric swallowed hard.

"A wave threw me on top of the rocks, clear of the water. I saw him trying to swim to where I was, to safety, then another wave hit. And that's the last time I saw him, until . . . on the beach . . ." Her lips trembled uncontrollably.

Eric could stand it no longer. He dragged her into his arms, squeezing her to him, resting his head on hers as if she were a prized possession.

Her tears continued. "I'm so sorry, Eric. So sorry that your father died. If there was anything I could do to change it, I would. If I could die in his place —"

"Don't say that!" he commanded, his arms drawing her even tighter.

"But *I* was the one on the beach. *I* was the one who didn't see the wave. Why did he have to die instead of me? It doesn't seem fair, Eric! Not to me. Look at all the children he left behind, and what all of you went through without him."

Eric heard the tortured passion of her words. He knew that this wasn't the first time she had thought them. In all the years, he had never once considered what the tragedy must have looked like through her eyes.

"Hush . . . hush," he repeated, trying to soothe her. For the first time he realized that she had been just as traumatized by the event as he and his siblings had, and his heart filled with empathy. "It doesn't matter anymore, Robin. What happened in the past has to stay in the past. We can't change it. We can't make it be anything other than what it was. My father . . . My father did what he had to do. He didn't have any other course open to him. That was the kind of man he was. To stand by when someone — particularly a child — was in trouble would have been completely out of character for him. And he accomplished what he set out to do. If he hadn't saved you . . . I don't want to think about if he hadn't saved you!"

She tightened her arms around his midsection and buried her face even deeper in his chest, her tears dampening his skin.

He continued, sensing that she needed to

hear him put his thoughts into words. "It's like . . . you're a gift he gave to me all those years ago, only I was too blind to see it. I blamed you, I blamed him . . . because I didn't get to tell him goodbye."

She lifted her head, and her beautiful dark brown eyes, washed by tears, alive with love, searched his face. "Would that have helped?" she whispered.

"I think it might. It might have helped all of us."

"It doesn't make the pain easier. We knew my dad was going to die, and when the time came . . ." She bit her lip. "I'm going to have to tell you about my dad sometime. He wasn't the kind of man you thought him to be. He was thoughtful and kind and . . . generous."

"I've spent a lot of years being angry with the wrong people, haven't I?"

"You've spent a lot of years being good to people, too. Your brothers and sisters . . . they're all nice human beings."

"A credit to all humanity," he teased, trying to lighten the tension.

Her smile was watery. "How would you feel about doing it again someday? Or are you all fathered out?"

He reached for a tissue from his bedside table and tenderly blotted her cheeks. "Are

you proposing what I think you're proposing?"

"I'm proposing, yes," she responded.

He captured her chin between his forefinger and thumb, looked deeply into her eyes
and said softly, "I accept," then lowered his
head and claimed her lips in a kiss that tried
to impart how desperately he loved her and
needed her and wanted her for all of time.

EPILOGUE

Sounds of the inn coming slowly to life barely penetrated the tanscendent world Robin and Eric inhabited as they sat at the dining room table, holding hands and gazing into each other's eyes.

Robin had never been so happy in her life. All the clouds that had followed her for so many years had disappeared. She could think of the future. Make plans. Plans that included Eric.

"I love you, Robin Farrell," he said softly, earnestly, using her correct last name.

"You say that so easily now."

"McGrath . . . Farrell. It doesn't matter. It's you I love, not your name."

"How do you think the others will feel?"

"About what?"

"Us. Being together. Getting married."

"They'll ask why it's taken us so long."

"They already know the answer."

"They'll still ask."

"I'm an only child, you know."

His brow lifted quizzically. "What does that have to do with anything?"

"Maybe I'm marrying you for your family."

"That's better than *not* marrying me because of them."

Robin remembered what Donal Caldwell had once said about Eric's potential brides being scared off by his large family. "Has that happened to you before?" she asked. She was curious to know if he had ever come close to marrying anyone else.

"Is that a roundabout way of asking if I've ever been in love before?"

"Yes," she answered honestly.

"I've been close a couple of times. One didn't like kids. The other — it just didn't work out. I liked her, but not enough to live with her for the rest of my life, or she with me."

"She must have been insane," Robin teased.

"She merely overlooked my more sterling qualities. Are you jealous?"

"No," Robin said archly. But she was, and he knew it.

"What about you?" he asked.

"The same. A couple of possibilities. I *wanted* to be in love more than I actually *was* in love."

"What stopped you?" he asked.

She smiled. "I must have been waiting for you."

Eric chortled at her answer and had started to kiss her when Samantha pushed through the swing door.

Eric and Robin jumped apart like guilty schoolchildren. Then, looking merrily into each other's eyes, they dissolved into laughter.

"Eric?" Samantha said, confused. But as she registered Robin's presence, she said in happy disbelief, "Robin! When did you get here? You're going to stay, right? But of course you are! You're —" She made a sweeping motion that took in their closeness and beaming smiles. "Oh, I'm so glad! I have to —" She hurred out of the room just as quickly as she entered it.

"The cat's well and truly out of the bag now," Eric said. "Give her five minutes and everyone in the place will know everything."

"It will save us having to make an announcement."

He grinned. "Do you want a big wedding?"

"Not particularly. Do you?"

"Not particularly."

"When?"

"As soon as possible."

Robin thought for a moment and started to count off people to invite. "We want your brothers and sisters there —"

"All we have to do is give them the date and the time. How about tomorrow?"

"— and a few of my friends. Not to mention my mother! A new dress. And what about Bridget? Wouldn't she feel slighted if we don't wait for her to get back?"

"Can you arrange all this by the Saturday after next? Bridget's due back that Friday."

"You're certainly in a hurry!"

"I've got you, I don't want to lose you."

Robin caught his cheeks between her hands. "Eric, you don't have to worry. You won't lose me. I don't plan to let you out of my sight!"

He knew what she was saying. She understood his family and the fear that secretly guided so much of their lives.

"It's what I want," he said huskily. "You're what I want. You're all I want."

Then, unable to resist the sweetness so near at hand, he kissed her with all the love that poured freely from his heart.

ABOUT THE AUTHOR

Ginger Chambers has been published by Harlequin Books since 1983. She has written for the Harlequin Superromance, Harlequin Everlasting Love and Harlequin American Romance lines. Before writing for Harlequin Books, she wrote for Dell Publishing in the Candlelight Romance, Candlelight Ecstasy and Candlelight Ecstasy Supreme lines. A native-born Texan, Ginger now lives in California.